I0736518

Tristan

TWILIGHT FALLS BOOK SIX

A.M. SALINGER

COPYRIGHT

Tristan (Twilight Falls #6)
Copyright © 2023 by A.M. Salinger
All rights reserved. Registered with the US Copyright Office.
Second paperback edition: 2024
ISBN: 978-1-9162270-4-0

www.AMSalinger.com
shop.adstarrling.com

Edited by www.ElfwerksEditing.com
Cover Design by A.M. Salinger

CHAPTER ONE

Fuck.

James Lang glared at the engine compartment of his Jaguar.

What he knew about cars could be written on the back of a stamp. Which was terribly unfortunate considering he was currently stuck on the side of a deserted mountain road and the sun was starting to set. He took his cell phone out, scowled when he saw the engine oil stain on his three-hundred-dollar Armani pants, and checked for a signal.

For the tenth time, the device returned—

"Nothing," James muttered under his breath in disgust. "Not a single fucking bar." His knuckles whitened on his cell. "I'm gonna kill Roman."

Roman Campbell was his best friend and the lead singer of Crazyknot, the world famous rock band James managed. Eighteen months after coming out of rehab and twelve months since Crazyknot made one of the most shockingly successful comebacks the music industry had ever witnessed, Roman had stunned James and the other members of their band by buying a dilapidated property in Twilight Falls.

Nestled in a forested valley in the San Bernardino Mountains, the picturesque town was a popular haven for tourists in summer and winter alike, its location ideal for outdoor sports enthusiasts as well as those interested in the gentler pace of life it offered.

James first visited the place two months ago, on Carter Wilson's wedding day. The A-list Hollywood star was a good friend of his from L.A. and a native of Twilight Falls. It was there that Carter had met and fallen head over heels in love with Elijah Davis, a Michelin star pastry chef who'd relocated from Paris to open a local bakery and eatery.

Carter and Elijah's wedding had been an elegant yet simple affair, the venue they'd chosen a wonderful backdrop to the heartfelt ceremony where they'd pledged their vows to one another.

Roman had also been a guest at the wedding. Unbeknown to James, the rockstar had spotted a 'For Sale' sign for a property on his way to the venue.

He'd showed up on James's doorstep with a rental RV that morning, put James's car on a trailer next to his Ducati, and driven them all the way to Twilight Falls to show him his new pride and joy.

Though James had told Roman he was crazy when he'd seen the run down home his best friend had purchased, he couldn't deny the attraction of the place. Originally built by an eccentric millionaire in the roaring 1940s, the rambling Colonial mansion stood on a rise at the end of a winding, graveled road, in the midst of ten acres of private woodland. With its ivy and wisteria covered facade and pretty leaded windows, the main residence had an undeniable charm that was visible even through the decades of grime that covered it. It even boasted its own swimming pool, tennis court, and guest house.

James had stayed with Roman throughout his meeting with his architect that morning, not because he didn't trust Roman to manage his own affairs, but because the rockstar had insisted on getting his opinion on the renovation plans. Though James hadn't shown it, he'd been impressed with the blueprints he'd seen and the 3d renderings Roman's architect had shown them on her computer.

Roman had made him lunch after she'd left.

"Your cooking skills have improved," James had told Roman tartly after taking a bite of the sandwich the rockstar had prepared for him.

Roman had sighed. "It's a pastrami sandwich, James. Even I can't fuck that up."

James had raised an eyebrow. "You seem to forget that I've known you since you were sixteen. Surely, you haven't forgotten *M&G Day?*"

Roman had rolled his eyes so hard they'd almost disappeared into the back of his pretty head. *M&G Day*, AKA mustard and gherkin day, was the infamous day the kids at their orphanage had been tasked with making lunch for the staff. It had been a comically epic disaster, the icing on the cake that had caused all the staff to groan at the awful sandwiches Roman had made. They had consisted of mustard and gherkins on soggy bread, and little else.

"You'll make a good wife yet," James had grunted at Roman after they'd finished the meal.

Roman had thrown a dishtowel at him.

It was late afternoon when they'd taken James's car off the trailer so he could make the drive back to L.A. He'd hugged Roman and dropped a kiss on his forehead as he'd gotten ready to leave.

"Call me if you need anything."

Roman's face had softened, the light in his eyes turning melancholic. "I'm okay, James. I'm much stronger than I was two years ago. And I have you and the other guys to thank for that." He'd squeezed his arms tightly around James. "I won't break again, I promise."

James had swallowed the sudden lump in his throat. He'd almost lost Roman once. And not just him. All of Crazyknot had. The other band members were from the same orphanage Roman and James had ended up in during their teens and the bonds between them had only gotten stronger with time. There was little they wouldn't do for one another.

He'd bidden Roman goodbye and left. That had been an hour ago.

And now, here I am, with a broken down car in the middle of nowhere. Guess there won't be a knight in shining armor coming to save me.

A self-disparaging chuckle left James then.

He wasn't exactly a damsel in distress. And no knight in shining armor would ever rescue him, physically or metaphorically. He'd come to terms with that a long time ago. After all, he was the Ice Princess of the music industry.

A wave of bitterness washed over James. He'd discovered he was attracted to guys a long time ago. He'd never had trouble sleeping with men until that awful night, seven years ago. He'd tried toys, sex clubs, and even watched porn, but to no avail. His few attempts at a one-night stand had all ended in disaster and he'd walked out of the hotel embarrassed and frustrated.

I should see a therapist.

An all too familiar, crushing sense of shame weighed him down at that thought. Seeing a therapist would mean confessing what had happened that night and the sordid circumstances that had led to it. He still wasn't ready for that. And he may never be. James ran a hand through his hair and grimaced.

Christ, the reporters in L.A. would have a field day if they discovered THE James Lang was frigid.

He was aware of his disagreeable reputation in the music industry. After all, it was one he'd carefully cultivated over the years, to protect himself and Crazyknot from the sharks that were bound to circle them as they shot to fame. It was all too easy for a young band to become tainted by the dark undercurrents of their industry. By deals done behind closed doors and unscrupulous people who would take advantage of them.

James had fought tooth and nail over the years to make sure Roman and the other members of

Crazyknot never became the targets of such dire intrigues. And there had been plenty of them, most of which his friends had been unaware of.

He studied the darkening sky and was debating leaving his car and walking down the mountain until he got better signal on his phone, when the sound of an engine reached his ears.

Thank God!

Relief made him weak. He hadn't realized how nervous he'd been.

The noise grew to the roar of a powerful motorbike. A headlight lit up the trees on the embankment to his right.

A black and silver Harley rounded the corner a moment later.

It was being ridden by a mountain of a man in a vintage brown leather jacket, dark gray jeans and boots, and a helmet with an opaque visor.

All of James's instincts went on high alert.

The guy shot past the car, slowed to a crawl, and did a U-turn before coming back up the slope.

James's palms grew sweaty when the stranger stopped his motorbike a short distance away. Even though it had started to grow dark, he could see the tattoos running up the side of the man's neck. He told himself he was being an asshole for making assumptions about the guy based on his appearance and stood his ground as the latter climbed off his Harley.

Then the stranger took his helmet off and all of James's instincts told him he'd been right.

This man was trouble with a capital T.

But not for the reasons James had presumed he would be.

Though he looked to be about the same height as James, the stranger was built like a brick house, with muscles to spare. He had short-cropped black hair, rich brown eyes, and dark stubble that framed an angular jawline, adding to his overpowering masculine presence.

James suspected that the tattoos on his neck extended over a considerable area of his impressive body. The guy also looked oddly…familiar.

"You're having engine trouble?" the stranger said.

James blinked. His voice was like warm honey poured over whiskey.

It went straight to James's cock and brought his shriveled libido to life with a jolt.

CHAPTER TWO

TRISTAN HART'S GAZE SHIFTED FROM THE SMARTLY-dressed, dark-haired man studying him warily from behind bottle-green framed specs, to the open hood of the silver Jaguar parked on the side of the road.

"I can take a look if you want." He hooked his helmet on the handlebar of his Harley and took a step toward the stranger.

The guy startled and backed away.

Tristan stopped, awareness rippling through him.

There was more than just caution in the man's widening, green eyes. He detected shock, as well as a sizzle of something else. Something that raised the hairs on the back of his neck.

"It's okay," Tristan said slowly. "I'm a mechanic."

The guy blinked, a rabbit caught in headlights. "What?"

Tristan ignored his confused tone and motioned to the car. "If it makes you feel any better, I can bring my tow truck and take you to my shop instead. Might be faster if you just let me see what the problem is first. I might be able to fix it here and now."

The man finally seemed to snap out of the daze he'd fallen into.

"Sorry," he mumbled. "Sure, go ahead."

Tristan noted his flushed ears with interest. He headed for the Jaguar, poked under the hood for a minute, and turned to the stranger. He noticed the guy had kept his distance, like he was ready to bolt at the first sign of danger.

Tristan was used to people being cautious of him because of his size, but this was the first time someone had looked at him like he was going to jump them.

Seems he hasn't recognized me.

"Might starting it up?"

The man's brow furrowed. "That's the thing. It won't start."

"Humor me."

The man hesitated between getting behind the steering wheel and pressing the ignition button. The engine rumbled, whimpered, and died. He got out and joined Tristan in front of the open hood.

"Can you tell what's wrong with it?"

Tristan's lips twitched at his tone. He sounded like a mother hen worrying about one of her chicks.

"You have a broken alternator and a clogged fuel filter."

The guy squinted. "Is that common?"

He has real pretty eyes.

Tristan masked his growing fascination and rubbed his chin. "How long have you had the car?"

"Five years."

Tristan made a face. "Unless you've driven this thing like a monster, the alternator shouldn't have broken. You got an extended warranty?"

The guy sighed. "No. I always say those are for fools."

Tristan struggled to hide a smile. He had to agree with the man.

The guy ran a hand through his hair, oblivious to the trace of engine oil he slicked through his locks.

"How long will it take to fix the alternator and the fuel filter?" he muttered, his frustration evident in the tight lines of his jaw.

"I can't fix either. I'll have to replace them."

The guy looked like he'd been told he had a month to live. "And how long will *that* take?" he asked in a long-suffering voice.

Tristan's lips twitched again. "A couple of hours." He shrugged. "Once I get it to the shop, that is."

The guy fixed him with a suspicious stare. "You have the parts in stock?"

"I've got some experience with luxury cars."

He didn't need to know Tristan was one of the most sought-after mechanics in the state or that the list of clients waiting for his services was as long as his arm.

"How about I give you a ride to the shop so you can wait there?" Tristan suggested. "It'll be more comfortable than hanging around on this road in the dark."

The guy's expression grew even more doubtful.

"Relax," Tristan said lightly. "I'm not a serial killer."

"That's what a serial killer would say," the man retorted.

Tristan tilted his head, a faint smile playing on his lips. "You don't recognize me, do you?"

The guy hesitated. "To tell you the truth, I feel like I've seen you somewhere before."

"It wasn't on *America's Most Wanted*, if that's what you're thinking," Tristan drawled. "I was one of the best men at Carter and Elijah's wedding."

The guy's eyes rounded.

"Oh. You're one of the Terrible Seven," he blurted out.

Tristan winced. "Yes, I am, for my sins."

The guy flushed. "Sorry."

Tristan smiled. "It's okay. I'm Tristan. Tristan Hart." He offered the guy his hand.

The man looked at it blankly for a moment. The color highlighting his cheekbones deepened when he realized what he was doing.

He recovered and shook Tristan's hand. "Sorry. James. James Lang."

Electricity sparked along Tristan's nerve endings at the contact.

Whoa.

James stiffened, the way his lips parted and his breathing accelerated slightly a tell-tale sign he'd felt the same thing. The faintest hint of disappointment darkened his eyes when Tristan let go of his hand.

Tristan pretended he hadn't noticed and headed over to the Harley to get his spare helmet. "You should put your suit jacket on. It's gonna get chilly during the ride."

James faltered before nodding. He retrieved his jacket from the Jag, locked up, and joined Tristan. He chewed his lip as he studied the helmet Tristan handed him.

"It won't bite," Tristan said, poker-faced.

James narrowed his eyes a little and yanked the helmet over his head.

"Sorry. It's not an exact fit, but it's better than nothing. Here, let me." Tristan reached up and adjusted the straps under James's chin.

James froze when Tristan's fingers grazed his neck.

Tristan's belly clenched on a wave of more than just awareness. Attraction sizzled through his veins when he noticed the quickening pulse at the base of James's throat. He finished securing James's helmet and slipped his own back on, his face inscrutable.

It wasn't like him to have just an immediate reaction to a man.

But there was no denying what his body was telling him.

He wanted to do more than just fix James Lang's car.

Tristan forced that compelling realization to the back of his mind to ponder later, climbed on the Harley, and started the engine. The motorbike sank a little when James got on the back.

"You ever ridden a bike before?"

"No."

Tristan couldn't help smiling at the false bravado in James's voice.

"It would be best if you put your arms around me," he advised. "Just to be safe."

"Okay," James said reluctantly.

He wrapped his arms gingerly around Tristan's waist and clasped his hands over his midriff. His thighs framed Tristan's hips as his chest pressed up against Tristan's back.

Damn, he smells good.

It took all of Tristan's willpower not to shiver as James's heat and intoxicating scent enveloped him. His dick came to life with a vengeance, so much so he was grateful it was dark and he was facing forward.

"Hang on tight."

CHAPTER THREE

Tristan had been right. By the time they rode up to his shop on the outskirts of Twilight Falls, James was chilled to the bones. It helped somewhat with the erection he'd desperately been trying to hide for most of the trip.

"Give me a minute." Tristan climbed off the Harley, headed through the front door, and disappeared inside the dark garage.

The faint beep of an alarm system reached James.

He sighed, told his freshly revived and seriously eager cock to calm the fuck down, and got off the motorbike. He took his helmet off and studied the building they'd pulled up to curiously.

It was way nicer than any mechanic shop he'd ever been to before. Made almost exclusively of solid, dark gray steel and painted breeze block, it boasted two industrial roller doors and high aluminum louver windows running around the length and width of the garage.

It stood on its own separate plot at the end of an industrial estate and boasted a simple, orange sign lit up by lights above the main door. Scrolled across it in an elegant black font were the words *Hart's Autoshop.*

The muscles of James's inner thighs twinged a little as he walked to the back of the Harley and put the spare helmet in the luggage box. He wasn't used to mounting anything, motorbike or man.

James chided himself at that last thought. But then again, it was hardly surprising considering the shocking fact that he'd been one hundred percent turned on and ready to go during the entire ride here.

He wasn't sure why Tristan Hart pushed all his buttons in the right way. But there was no denying he was the first guy James's dick had shown a serious interest in in seven whole years. Holding on to Tristan's rock hard torso and experiencing his body heat through the leather jacket he'd hugged throughout the ride here had been sheer torture. It also had him fantasizing about all sort of filthy things.

He'd wondered what Tristan looked like naked and aroused. Whether his cock was thick and long, just like he imagined it would be. He'd even spent several painfully pleasurable minutes picturing how it would feel to be pinned under that hard body and have it plunder his own.

Was Tristan a rough lover? Would he pound his ass the way James had often dreamt of being taken? Hard and fast and brutal, like an animal in rut? Or would Tristan be gentle and attentive and slowly drive James's out of his mind with pleasure?

James cursed his own rabid imagination as he waited for Tristan to emerge from the garage.

For all I know, this guy is as straight as a ruler. The only thing he's probably ever dipped his wick in is pussy.

He frowned as an errant thought crossed his mind. The last thing he intended to do was ask Carter about the sexual orientation of one of his friends. Lights came on inside the building, distracting him. The main roller door swung up on smooth hinges.

He stared as the interior of *Hart's Autoshop* was revealed.

It was not what he'd expected either.

James was coming to realize that Tristan Hart was full of surprises.

The target of his lustful fantasies came out, took the Harley, and started pushing the motorbike inside. He stopped halfway and cast a quizzical look over his shoulder at James.

"You coming?"

The words were so inanely appropriate for the wicked thoughts that had filled James's mind he almost swallowed his tongue.

Tristan arched an eyebrow at the strangled sound.

James cleared his throat and followed, heat flooding his face.

Jesus, he probably thinks I'm some kind of moron!

He switched his attention from Tristan's perfectly-shaped butt to the inside of the garage. The walls and ceiling had been painted a dazzling white and the concrete floor whitewashed a pale gray. The surfaces reflected the bright, LED strips suspended from the roof at regular intervals, the fluorescent bars skipping the skylights in the ceiling.

James imagined Tristan wouldn't need the lights at all on a bright day.

Considering how dirty a mechanic shop could get, he was surprised at the choice in colors. But, however hard he looked, he couldn't see a single spot of engine oil or grease anywhere.

His gaze shifted to what had initially attracted his attention when Tristan had opened the garage door. Parked across the interior of the mechanic's shop were several luxury sports cars and motorbikes.

A sliver of anxiety shot through James.

"Please tell me this isn't one of those shops where stolen cars are stripped of their parts and sold off," he mumbled before he could help himself.

Tristan placed his Harley next to a window overlooking a warmly-lit office, turned, and looked James dead in the eye.

"We also deal in human organs, so I'd be careful what I say next if I were you."

James felt the blood drain from his face.

Tristan's shoulders trembled.

James squinted. "You asshole."

Tristan's eyes crunched up as he finally released the laughter he'd been holding back. "I mean, you clearly had that coming," he chortled.

James ignored the way his skin prickled at the tantalizing sounds Tristan was making. Everything this guy did turned him on. For some reason, this made him even more irascible.

"That was uncalled for," he said between gritted teeth.

"No, it wasn't."

Tristan's tone had James almost doing a double take. A veneer of steel underscored the mechanic's velvety smooth voice despite his amused expression. It was clear James's ill-considered words had struck some kind of chord.

James swallowed. It wasn't often someone challenged him when he was in one of his moods. But even he had the grace to admit when he was in the wrong.

"I'm sorry. I was out of line."

"You're forgiven," the mechanic drawled. "Now, how about you get yourself comfortable in the office while I go pick up your car?" He pointed at the brightly lit room visible through the window. "I've put the heating on, so you should be nice and cozy. There's a coffee machine and a refrigerator with cold drinks and snacks if you want a drink and a bite. Restroom's at the back." He indicated a door opposite his office. "The waiting room also has a complimentary vending machine."

James blinked, surprised. "Do all mechanic shops have complimentary vending machines?"

"I don't know about other garages, but some of my clients are…kinda high maintenance." A lazy smile curved Tristan's lips. "It helps to get some sugar in them when they get cranky."

James couldn't help but feel that Tristan had just firmly put him on his high maintenance list.

Considering the boorish way he'd been acting, he couldn't blame the man.

Tristan headed for a handsome, gray pickup truck with a trailer, stopped like he'd recalled something, and came over to James. He put his hand out, palm facing up.

James stared. "What?"

Tristan arched an eyebrow, his eyes twinkling with mirth. "Your keys. I need them if I'm going to bring your car back."

"Oh." James flushed and dug his key and fob out of his pocket.

Luckily, his dick had finally settled down and there was no sign of the erection he'd been sporting for the better half of the last twenty minutes. His skin tingled when his fingers grazed Tristan's hand, like it had done the first time they'd touched. He prayed Tristan didn't notice the way he gulped.

The mechanic climbed into his pickup and reversed out of the garage.

"I'll be back soon," he called out through the driver's window. He engaged the roller door with a remote on his fob and headed out into the night.

James blew out a heavy sigh and rubbed the back of his head, the tension singing through his body finally draining out of him. A wave of lassitude followed it. He eyed Tristan's office.

Might as well check it out.

CHAPTER FOUR

TRISTAN ACTIVATED THE REMOTE AND WATCHED THE roller door rise. It had only taken him an hour to get James's car back to his garage. Granted, he'd driven a little faster than he would normally have, but considering he knew the mountain roads around Twilight Falls like the back of his hand and it was the start of the weekend, he hadn't felt too guilty about it.

He drove his pickup inside his workshop, maneuvered the trailer so he could offload James's car where he wanted it, and turned the engine off.

Silence greeted him. He looked quizzically in the direction of his office.

He'd expected James to come out.

Tristan climbed out of the truck and headed over to the room.

He found James sleeping on the couch.

The guy had draped his jacket meticulously on a hanger on the coatrack and had fallen asleep while he'd been leafing through a car magazine. Tristan smiled.

Even the way the magazine had settled on his lap was perfect.

An empty cup sat on the coffee table, along with the neatly folded wrapper of an energy bar.

Tristan tucked his hands inside his jeans pockets and leaned a shoulder against the doorjamb, committed to taking his sweet time studying the man his body had so clearly responded to earlier.

Somehow, he had a feeling few people got to look at James Lang the way he was doing right now.

The man was attractive in the kind of way that would make women, and plenty of guys, curious about what lay beneath the impeccable suits he wore and the icy exterior he projected. His broad shoulders and wide chest tapered to a slender waist, the expensive shirt he wore showcasing his trim abs and subtle six-pack. Tristan could tell he worked out from the toned muscles he'd felt wrapped around his body during the ride here.

His gaze dropped to James's solid thighs and long legs. His dick stirred as he found himself wondering what they would feel like locked around his hips and waist.

Tristan's instincts told him James would get pretty wild in bed.

He reluctantly dragged his gaze up James's body and examined his chiseled features. He seemed much younger with his face relaxed in sleep and his brow free of the permanent frown that seemed to live there.

Tristan noted the slight shadows under his eyes for the first time.

He looks tired.

He decided against waking James up, went to fetch a blanket from the closet, and draped it lightly over the sleeping man's chest and lap. James didn't stir. Tristan stared.

I should probably take his glasses off.

He squatted in front of James and carefully slipped his specs off his face.

James blinked drowsily.

Tristan's breath caught. *His eyes really are beautiful.*

"Hey," James mumbled. A dazzling smile curved his lips. He leaned forward and kissed Tristan.

Tristan froze. James's lips were soft and sweet where he pressed them against his mouth. And that smile? It made Tristan's pulse jump and had his cock swelling all over again as sexual attraction slammed into him like a freight train.

I am SO screwed.

James's eyelids fluttered closed. He sighed and fell back into a deep slumber, heedless of the fact that he'd just made Tristan hot and very, very hard.

Tristan's heart pounded. He raised trembling fingers to his mouth, his erection doing press-ups behind the zipper of his uncomfortably tight jeans.

He could still feel James's breath on his lips.

Tristan swallowed when he realized he hadn't wanted him to stop.

He wasn't a monk by any means. He'd had his fair share of bed partners over the years and had dated plenty of guys in L.A. and even a few in Twilight Falls. But none of them had come even close to making him experience the immediate, magnetic pull he was feeling for the man in front of him. Truth be told, he'd never come up against a situation like this in his entire adult life.

Also, does he make a habit of kissing random guys in his sleep?

Somehow, Tristan knew the answer to that question was a hard no. James didn't look like the kind of man who flirted with perfect strangers. If anything, he gave the complete opposite vibe.

Well, at least I know he's into guys.

Tristan would be lying if he said that didn't please him. He frowned in the next instant.

He couldn't make a move on James, however much he wanted to explore where this attraction could lead. The one steadfast rule he'd never broken in the last twelve years was to avoid mixing business with pleasure.

Tristan swallowed a sigh, placed James's glasses on the coffee table, and quietly tidied up before heading out into his garage to work on the Jag.

***

JAMES CAME TO WITH A START. SOMETHING SLID DOWN his chest and pooled on his lap as he bolted upright on the couch.

It was a blanket.

James looked up and gazed blankly around the cozy office. He bit back a groan when he recognized where he was.

Shit. I can't believe I fell asleep.

He glanced at his watch and realized he didn't have his glasses on. They were on the coffee table in front of him. Someone, Tristan in all likelihood, had not only removed them and cleared up his mess, he'd also put a blanket over him.

Heat flooded James's face. The whole thing made him feel embarrassed and strangely vulnerable, two emotions he wasn't used to experiencing.

A sound distracted him. Faint music drifted over from the garage. James hesitated before rising to his feet. He slipped his glasses on, shrugged into his jacket, and folded the blanket into a perfect square before placing it on the couch. He crossed the office with determined steps and came out in Tristan's workshop, only to rock to a stop.

The mechanic was bent over the engine compartment of his car. He'd slipped on dark, blue gray overalls and was whistling softly to a rock 'n' roll song playing on a vintage radio on a bench.

James's gaze locked on Tristan's well defined backside like a laser. His lips parted hungrily, his libido jackknifing into life like he'd stuck his fingers in an electric socket.

That ass is illegal.

Tristan straightened, cleaned his hands on a rag, and turned around. He stilled when he spotted James.

"Oh. You're up." His mouth curved up. "Just in time too. I'm done fixing your car."

James blinked. Tristan's smile was doing strange things to his pulse.

God, what is wrong with me?!

"Hmm, thanks for the blanket." He rubbed the back of his head awkwardly as he headed over. "I'm sorry I fell asleep. I must have been more tired than I thought."

"You look better for it."

James startled a little at that.

Did he watch me sleep?

That question should have creeped him out. Except it didn't. If anything, he found it oddly...arousing.

CHAPTER FIVE

JAMES TOOK FIRM CONTROL OF HIS EMOTIONS AS HE stopped beside Tristan. He eyed his car.

"It's really all fixed up?"

Tristan dropped the key and fob in his hand. "Why don't you test it out?"

James nodded gratefully. He climbed inside the vehicle while Tristan shut the hood.

The Jaguar came to life with a smooth rumble.

"Wow," James murmured.

His car sounded like it'd had a whole makeover.

Tristan propped his elbows on the edge of the driver's window. "She's purring like a kitten."

James stared at him blankly before bursting out laughing.

Tristan gave him a look that was half amusement, half curiosity. "What?"

"I'm sorry, do folks around here still use that expression?" James finally managed between chortles.

Instead of being offended, Tristan grinned. "You

should hear some of the stuff we say around the campfire."

James chuckled. "How much do I owe you?"

A mysterious light flashed in Tristan's eyes. "Consider the bill settled."

James blinked. "What?" He furrowed his brow. "Wait, I hope this isn't because I'm Carter's friend."

Tristan shook his head, his smile turning mischievous. "Let's just say you've already paid me in spades."

James stared. "How?"

Tristan rubbed his stubbled chin in a move James was beginning to realize he found incredibly sexy. His pulse skipped several beats when the mechanic's hooded gaze dropped to his mouth.

"I wasn't gonna say anything, but you kissed me in your sleep," Tristan drawled. "That's more than ample reward for fixing your car."

James's eyes rounded. He opened and closed his mouth soundlessly before squealing, "I *what?!*"

Tristan's grin widened. "You kissed me. It was kinda sweet, actually."

James shuddered and dragged a hand down his face, mortified beyond words. "Damnit. I can't believe I did something like that!" He met Tristan's amused stare. "Shouldn't you be more upset?" he said accusingly.

Tristan shrugged. "Since I enjoyed it, no."

James's breath locked in his throat. There was no mistaking the interested light in Tristan's eyes.

"You—you enjoyed it?!" he stammered.

Heat flooded his face when he realized what he'd

said and how the words had come out. Eager. Desperate even.

If Tristan registered the yearning in James's tone, he gave no sign of it. Instead, he dipped his chin solemnly. "Very much so. And, in case this was even in doubt, I'm gay." He hesitated. "Unfortunately, I have a hard rule about mixing business with pleasure."

James swallowed the hard lump of disappointment lodged in his throat. "Oh."

Tristan started to straighten, his tense jawline telling James he was just as frustrated.

"Well, technically, I'm not really your client," James mumbled.

Tristan froze.

James's heart thrummed as he found himself the focus of a pair of intense brown eyes. He licked his lips. "Technically, I'm just some guy you found on the side of the road."

Tristan's gaze focused on James's mouth.

"So, you're saying you were a damsel in distress?" he said slowly, as if exploring that tantalizing idea.

"Something like that," James managed in a strangled voice.

Being the subject of Tristan's undivided attention was incredibly nerve racking.

Tristan arched an eyebrow. "And I'm your knight in shining armor?"

James startled at the words that so closely mirrored his own thoughts mere hours ago.

Tristan frowned a little, like he was debating with himself internally.

"Well, I guess I can't really argue when you put it like that," he finally said.

He cupped the back of James's neck, leaned inside the car, and took his mouth in a torrid kiss.

James's cock went from interested, to 'Please, fuck me now!' interested in a heartbeat. He grabbed on to Tristan's biceps and groaned at the power he sensed beneath his fingertips. Tristan's hooded gaze stayed riveted to James's own stunned one as he learned the contour of his lips with gentle, sweeping movements, his stubble grazing James's jaw. Then he worked his tongue inside James's mouth and James's sanity fled.

This kiss was like nothing he'd ever experienced before.

It swept over him like a summer storm, leaving him hot and shivering in its path. His skin grew tight and his nerve endings sparked and sizzled as Tristan lapped and sucked and teased his tongue.

Tristan's husky groan echoed in James's ears as he angled his head and deepened the kiss, his hand hot where he clasped James's head. Goosebumps exploded across James's flesh. His cock throbbed and pulsed out precum, his balls and spine tightening in a way that told him he was close to having an orgasm.

James wrenched his mouth free from Tristan's, shocked at the way his body was reacting.

He couldn't believe he'd almost come from a kiss.

Their heavy pants filled the space between them as they gazed into each other's eyes. The color brightening Tristan's cheeks told James he'd been just as affected by their kiss.

"If you're expecting an apology, you won't get one."

Tristan's gruff words had James stiffening.

"I wasn't," he blurted out. "I'm the one who initiated that kiss."

Tristan's face relaxed a little. He glanced at James's erection and grimaced. "Well, I do have to apologize for *that*. It's gonna be hard to drive in that state, pun unintended."

James flushed and groaned. "That was terrible. In fact, it was almost as bad as your 'purring kitten' comment."

Tristan grinned. He cocked his head to the side. "Do you regret it?"

James raised an eyebrow. "What, telling you you're bad at puns?" he teased.

Tristan sighed. "No. Do you regret the kiss?"

James chewed his lip and decided to be honest. "No."

This seemed to please Tristan. "Good."

The silence between them grew loaded with sexual tension once more.

"I'd better leave," James said reluctantly.

"Yeah," Tristan murmured just as unenthusiastically.

James swallowed. "Hmm, are you sure you don't want me to pay you?"

A sinful smile curved Tristan's lips. He brought his mouth close to James's ear. "Well, there *was* this one thing I wanted to do to you on the hood of your car," he said huskily.

James shivered, his skin prickling as Tristan's hot breath teased his shell. "Fuck."

"Yup, that." Tristan laughed and straightened. "Have a safe drive."

James put his seat belt on and drove out of the garage before he said or did something that would change both their minds. His chest tightened with a bone deep longing that left him shaken as Tristan's shop disappeared in the rear view mirror.

One thing he was certain of.

No man had ever made him feel like Tristan had done tonight.

And he'd likely never see him again.

CHAPTER SIX

JAMES FOUND HIMSELF RETURNING TO TWILIGHT FALLS less than a week later. He would love to confess it was for Tristan Hart, but he had bigger problems on his hands than the man who'd occupied his every waking moment and his dreams since that hot encounter in the garage.

He drove through the picturesque town and up now familiar mountain roads, and soon reached Roman's property. The rockstar had messaged him the code for his new security gate a couple of days ago. He punched it in and rolled up the driveway.

Movement caught his gaze when he pulled to a stop behind the RV.

Roman stood on the porch of the mansion with Drake Jackson, his builder and, judging from the way Roman acted around the guy, the man the rockstar was very much interested in.

Irritation shot through James.

He knew Roman and Drake had had a casual thing

at Carter's wedding. He'd been willing to turn a blind eye for one night since no paparazzi had been allowed at the venue, but the last thing Crazyknot needed right now was another scandal.

Irrespective of what Roman thought, Drake Jackson looked like a big one.

The pair came down the steps as James got out of the Jag.

"Hey." Roman walked over to give him a quick hug. He pulled back, his expression quizzical. "I wasn't expecting you. Is everything okay?"

"We need to talk." James paused and glanced at Drake. "In private."

Annoyance flashed across Roman's face. He crossed his arms.

"What's this about, James?"

James faltered. The stubborn light in Roman's eyes and his defensive tone made it clear he wasn't in the mood to indulge him.

A voice broke the taut silence.

"I was going to have dinner at a friend's house. You two want to tag along?"

James and Roman stared at Drake like he'd grown another head.

Drake arched an eyebrow. "Is it a Crazyknot thing?"

Roman squinted. "What is?"

"That look that says you're dealing with an idiot," Drake drawled.

That was all it took for the tension to drain out of the atmosphere.

Roman visibly relaxed. He punched Drake lightly on the arm. "That's mean."

Drake chuckled. "For real, you guys have that death stare down to a T."

James swallowed a sigh. Though he was grateful for Drake's intervention, he wasn't going to be able to have a serious conversation with Roman until the builder was out of the picture.

"Whose car are we taking?" he asked with all the enthusiasm of a man about to have his testicles removed.

"Why don't I bring Roman in my Jeep and you follow in the Jag?" Drake suggested.

James met the man's innocent stare with a frown.

Devious bastard.

***

"ARE YOU SURE YOU'RE OKAY?" HUNTER THOMSON asked for the tenth time.

"Yes," Tristan grunted.

"Said Tristan the Grizzly Bear," Hunter muttered.

Tristan took his eyes off the road and flashed a narrowed look at his best friend.

Hunter sighed. "Alright, I'll back off, Grumpy."

A companionable silence fell between them. Tristan's thoughts drifted to the beguiling man he hadn't been able to stop thinking about after their unforgettable kiss last week. His fingers clenched on the steering wheel.

There was no reason for him to feel disappointed at

James's silence. They'd not exchanged phone numbers or made any promises to keep in touch. If anything, James was likely respecting the boundaries Tristan himself had set.

That thought riled him even more.

"I thought you were getting a ride with Theo," he told Hunter in an attempt to distract himself.

"He'll be late. He has a meeting with his suppliers." Hunter fake pouted. "Christ, anyone looking at your face right now would think you didn't want to spend time with your bestie."

"My bestie is an idiot."

They engaged in their familiar game of sarcastic repartee and soon pulled up on the Batistas' driveway. There were several vehicles already there and more lining the quiet street the house faced.

Tristan's eyes flared when he saw the one car he didn't think he'd ever see again.

"I wonder who the Jag belongs to?" Hunter mused as he climbed out of the pickup.

Tristan swallowed and stayed silent. *What's he doing here?!*

He knew James was the manager of Crazyknot. He'd seen him with Roman Campbell at Carter and Elijah's wedding and had shamelessly checked out the group's bio after James left his garage last week. Most of the articles he'd seen about the rock band had mentioned James in one form or another. It was clear the manager was not only highly respected in the music industry, he was also seen as some kind of inflexible paragon of virtue.

Tristan's palms grew sweaty as he and Hunter trod a path they'd walked thousands of times before. Bar death or a dire emergency, Wyatt and Izzy Batista's home was where they all religiously came for dinner and a game of poker Wednesday nights. It was a tradition that stemmed from the visits they used to pay to Izzy and Wyatt's house when their parents had still been in town. Helen Batista loved cooking and the Terrible Seven had turned out to be the perfect testers and recipients for her larger than life meals.

Tristan knew Elaine Martinez had had a hand in organizing those initial togethers. Elaine was the mother of Miles Martinez, the one member of the Terrible Seven who hadn't made dinner and poker night at the Batistas in the last decade.

The victim of a horrific accident that had left him in a coma shortly after he'd turned eighteen, Miles was currently being taken care of in a private home in Twilight Falls. There was technically nothing wrong with Miles's brain. He just never woke up after the accident.

The guilt the rest of them had lived with since that fateful day had still not entirely faded. The drunk driver who had crashed his car into Alex's mom's truck had been well over the limit. It was nothing less of a miracle that Miles and the driver of the car were the only ones who'd been seriously injured in the accident. The rest of the Terrible Seven had walked out of the wreckage completely unscathed.

It was a cruel fate they had all long cursed. Because, of the Terrible Seven, Miles was the sweetest and most innocent of them all. To the point Alex and Hunter suspected he'd never been kissed before the accident.

The front door was open. They walked inside the Batista home to a merry brouhaha coming from the direction of the kitchen.

Hunter's face glazed over as he inhaled deeply. "We're having spaghetti and hot dogs. And Elijah's cooking."

Tristan made a face. "Your sniffer dog abilities worry me. Are you sure you're not part werewolf?"

Hunter flipped a finger at him. He put it away quickly when a little blonde girl came running out of the kitchen with ketchup and mustard smeared around her mouth.

Carter stormed out after her. "I said no more hot dogs, Maisie. Or there'll be no dessert for you."

The little girl dashed past Hunter and Tristan, giggling.

"Oh, hey," Carter greeted them distractedly as he disappeared down the corridor after his niece and adoptive daughter.

Hunter flashed a smug look at Tristan. "See, I was right."

Tristan rolled his eyes.

Maisie's delighted squeal reached them. She reappeared, firmly tucked under Carter's arm. The actor made a show of lifting up her onto his shoulders. She grabbed on to his head and beamed at Hunter and Tristan.

"Hi, Uncle Hunter! Hi, Uncle Tristan!"

"Hey, sweetie." Hunter rose and pressed a kiss to

Maisie's cheek. She giggled when Tristan repeated the greeting.

Tristan eyed Carter's slightly harassed expression. "You want a kiss too?"

Carter scowled. "Heck no!"

"Papa Carter's kisses are reserved for Papa Elijah," Maisie said with another giggle. "Auntie Izzy showed me how to steal hot dogs," she added proudly.

"Izzy!" Carter growled. He headed back into the kitchen, murder in his eyes.

"Did someone say my name?" A pretty brunette with green eyes poked her head out of a room to their right.

Tristan grimaced at Wyatt Batista's little sister. The unofficial eighth member of the Terrible Seven, Izzy had made their lives a merry hell since she was old enough to follow them around. Despite their grumblings, they wouldn't have it any other way.

"You showed the kid how to steal?" Tristan said.

Izzy squinted. "Steal is a strong word. I prefer 'being creative with one's hands.'"

"Are you hiding in there?" Hunter asked suspiciously.

"Oh, please," Izzy scoffed. "Like I couldn't take Carter with one hand tied behind my back. I'm wrapping Christmas presents."

"It's three months to Christmas," Tristan observed drily.

Izzy narrowed her eyes. "I like to be organized." A furtive look danced across her face as she glanced in the direction of the kitchen. She beckoned them closer, her expression turning conspiratorial.

Tristan and Hunter shared a puzzled glance and went over.

"Guess who Drake brought?!" Izzy hissed excitedly.

Tristan could guess plenty.

"The Grinch?" Hunter hazarded. "*Ouch!*"

Izzy had slapped him on the arm. "I swear I don't know what Theo sees in you."

Hunter grinned. "I have a smart mouth and a hot bod."

Izzy and Tristan eyed him dully.

Hunter's grin widened. "And he loves what my mouth does to his bod—"

"And there is it," Tristan grumbled.

"It's like his life would end if he went five minutes without uttering some kind of sexual innuendo," Izzy groaned.

"You guys are hurting my feelings," Hunter said drily. He arched an eyebrow at Izzy. "So, spill, Butterbeans. Who did Drake bring?"

Izzy decided to overlook her most loathed childhood nickname, too buzzed about the secret she was about to reveal. "Roman Campbell."

Hunter drew a sharp breath. "The rock star?! The guy who was at Carter and Elijah's wedding? The one who showed up at *The Watering Hole* last weekend and caused that uproar? *That* Roman Campbell?!"

Izzy hushed Hunter before continuing her story in a gleeful tone that almost made Tristan shudder. "Looks like Drake caved in and decided to take on the

Strickland Estate project after all." She leaned in close and waggled her eyebrows. "Although, between you and me, I think he and Roman are—"

A slight noise had Izzy pausing and staring over Tristan and Hunter's shoulders. Her face grew flustered for second before she smoothed out her features and directed a charming smile at whoever she'd just spotted. Tristan twisted on his heels. His pulse stuttered.

James had just come out of the kitchen.

He rocked to a stop when he saw Tristan and Hunter. "Oh."

CHAPTER SEVEN

The whole room groaned when Tristan laid his
cards out on the kitchen table.

"Read them and weep, suckers."

James narrowed his eyes. "Wait."

Everyone looked at James, including Tristan.

The mechanic's pinched expression told James he
was still annoyed about what had happened earlier in
the hallway, when James had greeted him like he was a
perfect stranger. James clenched his jaw.

*What did he expect me to do? It's not like I can tell his
friends he fixed my car and almost made me climax from a
kiss last week.*

Torrid images flashed through James's mind at that
last thought. His ears warmed up.

The drive back to L.A. the night Tristan had kissed
him had been sheer torture. All he'd wanted to do was
pull over on the side of the road and stroke himself to
his first orgasm in years. He'd barely made it home

before he'd yanked his zipper down and freed his throbbing dick. He'd leaned his back against his front door and finally given his raging cock the attention it deserved, all while still standing in the middle of his hallway.

It had only taken a handful of strokes for James to explode that first time, his climax so powerful he'd almost blacked out. The next four times had been more measured, especially the one in the shower where he'd thrust his fingers up his ass while he'd rubbed himself briskly, Tristan's face and powerful body at the forefront of his filthy fantasies.

He'd dreamt about the sexy mechanic every night since then and woken up with a boner most mornings. Having to give himself two to three handjobs a day to be able to even function normally had been a new experience for James. He'd never imagined he'd see the day when his life would be ruled by his hot and horny dick.

It was as if his body was making up for all his pent-up years and was intent on experiencing as many releases as he could give it. And give it he did, in all kinds of shockingly arousing places. The best one by far beside his kitchen table had been the garage. Stripping off and bending over the hood of his Jag to pleasure himself to two eye-watering orgasms while he'd imagined Tristan fucking him from behind had been down right one of the most carnal sexual acts he'd ever indulged in. He hadn't even felt sorry when he'd had to wipe down cum from his expensive car.

The expectant silence around James jolted him back to the present. The arrogant way Tristan arched his eyebrow at him across the table had his cock twitching to attention. He swallowed his irritation.

He disliked being so sensitive to this man's every move.

James fixed the mechanic with a bold stare and spread his cards on the table.

Tristan froze. His eyes widened a little.

"Son of a bitch." Admiration dawned on Hunter's face. "He has a full house!"

Delighted roars erupted across Wyatt Batista's kitchen.

"Is this the first time Tristan's lost by any chance?" Nathan Hardy asked Theo Miller.

Theo sipped his beer, his expression amused as he studied Tristan's stony face. "Sure looks that way."

Roman looped an arm around James's shoulders.

"I told you you could beat him," the rockstar said smugly.

James spotted Drake's annoyed stare.

Looks like someone doesn't like it when Roman touches another guy.

"I would be more impressed if we were playing with real money instead of game tokens," he said half-heartedly.

Tristan furrowed his brow. "Not all of us are filthy rich."

Hunter glanced at Tristan, surprise flashing in his gaze.

James's stomach knotted on a wave of embarrassment and anger. He hadn't meant to come across as a superior asshole. Besides, he knew from looking Tristan up that he wasn't exactly a poor man. *Hart's Autoshop* was among the top five rated mechanic shops in the state and its website boasted testimonials from several big Hollywood names.

Roman frowned at Tristan. His mouth parted.

Izzy Batista walked inside the kitchen with Carter before the rockstar could come to James's defense.

"What'd we miss?" she said breezily.

Alex Hancock grinned. "James beat Tristan."

Izzy's jaw dropped. "No way!" She stared from Tristan to James and back again, her eyes round.

Color stained Elijah's cheeks a pretty pink when Carter took the seat beside him and pulled him onto his lap.

"Carter, we're with company!" he berated in a low voice.

"I see your honeymoon period is still in full flow," Izzy noted acerbically.

"It's never gonna end," Carter declared with a confident grin that had Elijah blushing even harder. With their adopted daughter Maisie sleeping soundly upstairs, the actor had been granted free rein to act out his feelings toward his new husband.

James's chest twinged as he gazed at the happy couple. They weren't the only ones settled in loving relationships. Hunter and Theo. Wyatt and Nathan.

It was evident over half the men in the room were insanely happy with their love lives.

"Yeah, yeah, everyone's having sex," Izzy grumbled. "Except for me and Tristan." She pursed her lips. "The jury's still out on Drake."

Drake smiled and stole a glance at Roman from under his lashes as he wordlessly drank his beer.

James frowned.

It wasn't until a while later that he finally managed to catch Roman alone for the first time that evening.

Roman startled a little when he came out of the downstairs restroom and found James lurking in the corridor.

"Oh, hey." He relaxed and smiled. "There's a bathroom upstairs too."

A muscle jumped in James's cheek as he glared at Roman.

"Are you and Drake fucking?" he grated out.

Remorse immediately followed his harsh words. It wasn't what he'd meant to say. Seeing Tristan tonight had rattled him and almost made him forget why he'd come to Twilight Falls in the first place. Still, lashing out at his best friend hadn't been number one on his plan of action tonight.

Roman sucked in air. "What?"

James clenched his fists, intent on getting the answer now that he'd asked the question. He needed to plan for the worst eventuality.

"I said, are you and Drake—?"

"I heard you the first time!" Roman snapped. He grabbed James's arm and dragged him down the hallway and inside Wyatt's den. He whirled around to face James. "What the hell is wrong with you?!"

James swallowed and scowled. "I'm worried about you."

Roman made a frustrated sound and threw his arms in the air. "You're always worried about me! It doesn't mean I'm going to stop living my life just to make you happy, James!"

James's stomach lurched at Roman's angry expression. He had to remind himself he was doing this for Roman's own good.

"Drake being your contractor makes any kind of relationship between you a conflict of interest, Roman. He of all people should know that!"

Fury darkened Roman's eyes. "What, are you my lawyer now?! And FYI, I'm the one who wanted us to sleep together!"

James's stomach plummeted. "So, you *are* sleeping with him!"

"We've slept in the same bed, but we haven't have sex," Roman said between gritted teeth. "Not that it's any of your damn business, James!"

James flinched.

Roman looked like he was about to reach out to him. He stopped himself at the last second and drew a shaky breath. "The lights went out at the estate during the storm last night," he confessed in a low voice. "I was having a full-blown panic attack when Drake found me. He drove me to his place and took care of me."

James inhaled sharply.

"Why didn't you call one of us?!" he blurted out, unable to hide the pain in his voice this time around.

Though rehab had cleared Roman of his addiction

to drugs and alcohol, he hadn't completely come to terms with his dark past and the reason for his panic attacks. Guilt seared James. He was the one Roman always called when he was suffering from one of his episodes.

Shit! Have I become so unreliable?!

He ground his teeth. What he needed to tell Roman was only going to make things worse.

"My phone died," Roman admitted guiltily.

All of James's concerns were swept away by the sudden wave of fear and fury that overwhelmed him at the sheer stupidity of the man looking at him sheepishly. He cursed colorfully.

Roman winced. "Look, I get it. I get that you're worried that I'll screw up again and make the band suffer because of my—"

"That's not why I'm worried about you, goddammit!" James roared, his patience finally snapping under the riot of emotions storming his heart.

He shuddered when Roman rocked back on his heels, his face ashen.

Fuck! Why am I taking out my frustration on him?!

A fraught silence befell them.

"What's really going on, James?" Roman's voice was full of dread, his expression telling James he'd finally clocked on that something serious was going on. "This isn't like you at all."

James stayed silent for a moment as he put his tumultuous thoughts together.

This was not the way this should have gone.

He took a deep breath, raked his hair with a hand, and finally spoke.

"It's your dad, Roman," James said dully. "I heard from our lawyers today." His stomach twisted as he met Roman's dazed stare. "He's out on probation."

CHAPTER EIGHT

ALL THE BLOOD DRAINED OUT OF ROMAN'S FACE. THE rock star's breath left his lips on a guttural rasp as he bent over, struggling to draw air.

Alarm filled James. "Roman!"

"Roman?"

James looked over his shoulder.

Drake was standing in the doorway of Wyatt's den. His eyes darkened with fury when he registered Roman's terrified expression. He strode inside the room and grabbed James by the neckline of his shirt.

"What the hell did you do to him?!"

James wrapped a hand around Drake's wrist and tugged, remorse making his touch more savage than he'd intended. "I didn't do anything to him. I just gave him some bad news!"

Roman swallowed convulsively. "It's my dad. My dad's out of jail!"

Drake let go of James, stunned. "What?"

He brushed past James and embraced Roman.

Roman shuddered against Drake's chest. "That's why James came over," he mumbled. "To tell me about my dad."

Drake squeezed him tightly. His gaze found James, his anger replaced by a mixture of concern and dread. "How is that possible? I thought he was doing time for embezzlement."

Jealousy speared James at the way Roman clung to Drake. He scowled, his tone turning accusing. "He knows?"

"I told him last night," Roman murmured with a trace of defiance.

"Fuck." James clenched and unclenched his fists. "The bastard got out on good behavior," he finally grated out. He clocked Roman and Drake's stunned expressions and grimaced. "Yeah, I don't believe it either."

"He doesn't know where Roman is, does he?" Drake asked stiffly.

James shook his head. "No. And he's banned from making any kind of contact with Roman or talking about Roman to the press." He paused. "But he might still try and get to him."

"Because of his money?" Drake said harshly.

"That. And—" James stopped.

"And because he thinks I'm his property," Roman finished in a lifeless voice.

Tristan came out of the kitchen and headed down the hall to the restroom. Low voices reached him from Wyatt's den. He slowed when he recognized James's voice.

"I'm sorry, Roman," the manager was saying in a tone raw with regret. "I'll take care of this, I promise."

"Let's get you home," Drake murmured. He came out of the room, his face tight and his arm wrapped protectively around a pale-faced Roman. He stopped when he saw Tristan.

"Something's come up," he said stiltedly. "Can you give Izzy and Wyatt our apologies?"

"Sure," Tristan murmured impassively. He'd rarely seen Drake so strained.

He followed the couple with his gaze as they headed out of the house. It was clear as day that something was going on between them.

James exited the den next. He rocked to a halt when he registered Tristan's presence, surprise widening his pupils for a moment. Tristan's chest tightened.

James looked even more haggard than Roman.

"I'm sorry," he mumbled, not quite meeting Tristan's eyes. "Please give Izzy and Wyatt my regards." He brushed past Tristan and made for the front door.

Tristan frowned as it closed after the manager.

What the hell happened in there?

Izzy popped her head out of the kitchen. "Did someone leave?"

"Yeah," Tristan said slowly. "Drake, along with Roman and James. They said something came up."

"Oh." Izzy's face fell. "I was gonna grill Drake about Roman."

Tristan grimaced. "Why doesn't that surprise me?"

Poker night officially ended a half hour later. Tristan waved the others goodbye as they got in their respective vehicles and headed out into the night.

It only took fifteen minutes for him to reach his house. Located on the shore of a small lake on the western outskirts of Twilight Falls, the two-story lodge stood in its own clearing at the end of a private road.

The log and glass cabin was his pride and joy, not just because he'd helped Drake build it from scratch six years ago. It was the kind of forever home he'd always envisioned himself living in one day.

He'd figured it would be an unattainable dream. But his business had done incredibly well from the get-go and demand for his services was such that he'd had a waiting list of eager clients within his first year of opening up *Hart's Autoshop*. He'd had to take on extra staff in his second year of business and now had five other mechanics working for him.

The only thing missing from his picture perfect life was someone to share it all with. James's face flashed before Tristan's eyes at that last thought. He furrowed his brow.

Jeez, I've only kissed the guy once.

His cock stirred accusingly as he relived the numerous times he'd rubbed himself to a powerful orgasm while thinking of that particular kiss and the man he'd stolen it from. Judging by the way his body had reacted to James's presence tonight at Wyatt and

Izzy's place, the attraction he'd felt for the guy hadn't been a fluke.

Tristan took the last corner on his driveway and stepped on the brakes a little harder than he would normally do when his home came into view.

A silver Jaguar was parked in front of the lodge.

Surprise and a sliver of anticipation quickened his pulse when his gaze found the man on his porch.

James sat on the wooden swing looking out over the lake, his elbows on his knees and his shoulders slumped under the soft glow of the external lights. He looked up when Tristan parked next to his car.

Though his face was cast in shadows, Tristan could tell he was hurting from the rigid lines of his body. He stepped out of the pickup and closed the door.

"How did you find my place?"

A sigh shuddered out of James at his light tone. "I thought you'd be more upset."

Tristan shrugged. "I'm not. I'm just curious."

He headed up the steps, crossed the porch, and leaned a hip against the railing opposite the swing. Somehow, he had a feeling James needed the space right now.

"Did you ask Carter?"

James grimaced and rubbed the back of his neck awkwardly. "Yeah."

Tristan smiled faintly. "Good choice. He tops my list of people least likely to blab about sensitive matters, along with Elijah."

James's lips quirked briefly. "Let me guess. Izzy is at the bottom of that list?"

"Her and Hunter both," Tristan drawled. "And I say that as the guy's best friend."

A low chuckle left James.

The sound danced down Tristan's spine and made the attraction that existed between them sizzle across his skin. He wanted to go over to James and test it out, but decided to stay put. He doubted he'd come here without an agenda. The man was far too cautious for that.

James's smile faded. A haunted look darkened his eyes to a stormy sea green.

The taut silence that stretched between them was broken by the sound of waves lapping gently at the shingles on the shore.

"What happened back there?" Tristan said quietly.

James hesitated. He swallowed. "I can't tell you the details. But it might make things…tense around here for a while."

Tristan read between the lines. "You mean, around Roman and Drake?"

James nodded. His shoulders drooped a little more, as if another weight had been added to them. He lowered his gaze to the floor.

A stark realization shot through Tristan then. His stomach clenched.

He'd never seen someone look as lonely as James did in that moment.

Though it was evident the man was blessed with great friends and wealth, he cut a forlorn figure where he sat dejected on Tristan's porch.

It was becoming apparent to Tristan that James was

a man with many secrets. Secrets he'd had to carry on his own for a long time.

Tristan's instincts told him it was for the sake of the people he cherished the most. He asked the question that hung unspoken between them.

"Why are you here, James?"

James flinched. His knuckles whitened where he clenched his fists on his knees.

Tristan finally moved. He squatted in front of James and tilted his chin up gently with a knuckle. What he saw twisted his gut and had his breath locking in his throat.

Tears glittered on James's eyelashes. His mouth quivered.

He looked like a man on the brink of a breakdown.

Tristan's heart pounded as he gently removed James's glasses and tucked them inside the breast pocket of his pristine suit. He swept a thumb at the corner of James's right eye, wiping away a hot tear. He would analyze the emotions raging through him later. Right now, there was something more urgent that needed his attention.

His instincts had given him the answer James wouldn't.

Because it wasn't just pain and frustration and dread he could see on James's face. Bottled up behind the man's rigid self-control was an emotion he was trying to fight.

"Tell me what you want me to do, James."

Tristan grazed James's lips with his finger. For a moment, he wondered if he'd gotten it wrong.

The way James's pupils dilated told him he hadn't.

Tristan saw the dam holding back the storm inside James finally break. He took a ragged breath, grasped Tristan's face, and kissed him with a passion that made Tristan's dick come to life in an instant.

Tristan slipped his fingers in James's hair and returned the kiss just as ardently. Their lips and tongues melded together hungrily for a timeless moment, their hooded gazes locked on one another as they each learned what the other liked.

James finally pulled back and pressed his forehead to Tristan's.

"Make me forget," he mumbled, his eyes blazing with need and his skin burning hot where he touched Tristan. "Make me forget everything."

CHAPTER NINE

TRISTAN STILLED. JAMES'S PULSE RACED AS HE GAZED into the dark eyes opposite him, unable to read beyond Tristan's inscrutable stare for a moment.

His throat tightened.

He still couldn't believe he'd come here. That he was asking Tristan to do something the man had stated he would never do.

This is crazy. James inhaled shakily. *I should just leave.*

"If we do this, I can't fix your car again," Tristan said gruffly.

James stared, surprise overriding his tumultuous thoughts. "What?"

Tristan leaned in and nipped at his lower lip with strong, white teeth. Desire knotted James's belly at what he read on Tristan's face.

"That would definitely make you my client," Tristan muttered, his scalding gaze focusing on James's mouth.

James shuddered. Tristan was giving him a way out. His chest lightened.

He wants this too. But he's letting me make the final call.

For once in his life, James decided to throw caution to the wind and do something he really wanted. Something he craved.

"Deal," he whispered.

Lust turned Tristan's expression feral.

James shivered. Tristan looked like he wanted to eat him alive.

A moan left him when Tristan ducked his head and pressed his lips to the hollow of his throat. He closed his eyes, stunned by how much pleasure he derived from that simple kiss.

"I hope you won't regret this," Tristan murmured hotly against his skin.

He bit down gently.

James gasped at the light sting and the way Tristan's stubble scratched his flesh. His breathing quickened. He squirmed a little, his pants growing uncomfortably tight where his erection stretched the material. "I won't."

"Good." Tristan took his mouth in a scorching kiss and pulled him to his feet.

Blood pounded in James's ears as Tristan led him inside the lodge. His skin felt tight and his body burned.

Gone was the fear he'd always lived with. The fear that he would be unable to have an orgasm while sleeping with another man. All it would take to get him off right now was Tristan's touch. He could feel the tight self-control he'd always exerted over his emotions slipping away as he arrived at a startling truth.

He could be his true self with Tristan.

James swallowed as he registered the warm, masculine decor of the hallway they were navigating. He tugged on Tristan's hand.

"Here." He licked his lips and glanced around. "I want you to make me come here first."

Tristan's pupils dilated at the bold command. He turned, the color staining his cheekbones and the bulge in his jeans indicating he liked that idea. He clasped James's waist and walked him backward until he had him trapped against his front door.

"Why do I get the feeling you've planned this out?"

Tristan's husky voice raised goosebumps on James's skin. He shivered when Tristan nudged his chin up with his nose and rained hot kisses down the column of his throat.

"That night we first kissed? I came in my hallway."

Tristan froze at his mumbled confession. A shudder shook him. He straightened and gazed heatedly at James.

James's heart pounded at the carnal light blazing in Tristan's smoldering eyes. He looked like he was about ready to bend him over and fuck him raw.

James's ass twitched at that filthy notion.

He'd never taken a man bareback before.

"Show me," Tristan growled. He took James's mouth in a kiss that made his head spin before stepping back. "Show me how you touched yourself that night."

James panted, so excited he just about vibrated with desire. He couldn't believe he was really about to do this. All it took was one look at the way Tristan was clenching his fists for James to realize he had nothing to fear.

Tristan wanted him, plain and simple.

He raised a hand to his belt. Tristan's gaze locked on his fingers like a laser beam.

The sound of the buckle being undone was loud in the fraught hush between them. James pulled his zipper down with trembling fingers and freed his aching cock.

Tristan's breathing accelerated as he stared at James's flushed erection.

"Do it," he ordered hoarsely. His hand dropped to the swelling in his jeans.

James started stroking himself while Tristan massaged his own cock. He bit his lip at the exquisite pleasure of performing this sinful act under Tristan's heated stare. An animal sound left Tristan as precum pearled on James's tip. He stepped closer, so close James's fingers brushed against his hand as they both fondled their rock hard shafts.

Tristan leaned in.

"This is hands down the most arousing thing I've ever seen," he whispered hotly in James's ear. He bit down gently atop the shell.

James groaned as his dick throbbed and pulsed. The sound turned to a gasp when Tristan ran a knuckle across his leaking head.

Tristan brought his finger to his mouth and licked the precum glistening on his skin, his dark eyes riveted to James's stunned gaze.

"Sweet and salty, just like I thought it would be," he rumbled.

Then he kissed James, dropped his hand to his naked cock, and took over pleasuring him.

James moaned raggedly as Tristan rubbed and teased his flesh with expert motions of his fingers. It didn't take long for his orgasm to gather at the base of his spine and tighten his belly. The hot ball of ecstasy building deep inside him exploded with a force that made him see stars.

James wrenched his mouth from Tristan's, grabbed onto his shoulders, and squeezed his eyes tight as he convulsed against him, head thrown back and lips open on a guttural cry. Tristan rained tender kisses on his throat as he writhed in his hold.

Sweat beaded James's face when he finally came down from the blistering high Tristan had brought him to. He blinked his eyes open dazedly.

Tristan smiled against his lips. "I think you passed out a little there, Mr. Lang."

James flushed at his teasing expression. He looked down and swallowed when he saw the cum filling Tristan's palm.

"We should clean that up."

Tristan pressed a quick kiss to his mouth, grabbed a tissue from a box on a console table, and wiped his hand clean. He took hold of James's wrist and tugged him deeper inside the cabin.

"Where else did you come while thinking about me?"

James finally took note of his surroundings as Tristan guided him through an airy, open lounge and kitchen-dining room overlooking the lake.

"Your place is unreal," he mumbled.

He didn't have to be an expert to know the furniture and decorative pieces he was looking at carried hefty price tags. Whoever had decorated Tristan's place had evidently been given carte blanche to do it up.

"Thank you, but that's not going to get you out of answering my question." Tristan's eyes flashed with a banked heat as he guided James up a glass and wood staircase.

James licked his lips. "The shower. My kitchen. And, hmm, over my car."

Tristan stopped in his tracks. "You gave yourself a handjob in your garage?"

The hungry way he stared at James told him he really wanted to see him perform that particular act.

"Yes," James confessed, his face hot. "Several times."

Tristan eyed James shrewdly as he paused on the landing.

James gasped when he yanked him close.

"What aren't you telling me?" Tristan nipped at his jawline.

James shivered and tilted his head, desire tightening his body like a bow all over again at the strength and passion in Tristan's touch.

Tristan accepted his silent invitation and kissed and nibbled on his neck.

"I—*Ah!* Fuck that feels good!" James moaned and pressed closer to Tristan when he feasted on the pulse beating wildly at the base of his throat. "I—I imagined you bending me over my car and fucking me from behind!"

An unholy growl left Tristan at this confession. He squeezed James's butt and molded their groins.

"Shit." He raised his head and took James's mouth ravenously as he ground their erections together. "It's a shame it's too chilly for us to do that."

James's dick twitched at that mental image. He sucked in air when Tristan hooked his hands under his thighs and lifted him up.

CHAPTER TEN

He wrapped his legs around Tristan's hips and closed his arms around his powerful shoulders.

"I love your body," James confessed as Tristan carried him up the stairs like he weighed nothing.

Tristan raised an eyebrow. "So, you're saying you like my muscles more than my dazzling personality and my brains?"

James could tell he was teasing. He pursed his lips and squeezed Tristan with his thighs.

"I like your dazzling personality and your brains just fine. But I've totally imagined being under you and having you crush me to a bed and pound my ass until I scream."

Tristan swore at that vivid depiction. His fingers found the cleft of James's butt.

James shuddered as he grazed his hole through the material of his pants.

"Is that how you want me to make love to you?"

Tristan growled against his mouth. "Do you want me to be rough?"

James moaned, his ass contracting hungrily. "I'll take you any way you want to give it to me." He slipped a hand between their bodies and tugged on Tristan's erection.

"Fuck!" Tristan hissed, his hips jerking.

He reached the end of a corridor, entered a dark room, and dropped James unceremoniously on his bed.

James's heart thundered against his ribs as he bounced on the inky sheets. He licked his lips and watched Tristan flick on a floor lamp. Tristan yanked the curtains across the glass wall and doors overlooking a balcony and the lake and pinned him to the bed with a blistering stare.

"Strip," he ordered in voice rendered harsh with lust.

James swallowed. He took off his shoes and tie, shrugged out of his jacket, and hooked his fingers in the waistband of his pants.

Tristan kicked his boots off and unbuckled his jeans.

James froze with his trousers halfway down his thighs when Tristan shrugged out of his leather jacket and yanked his T-shirt off.

He'd been dead on the money. Not only was Tristan's body everything he'd dreamt it would be, the tattoos on his neck flowed beautifully down his thick arms and across his powerful chest and back.

"Your hands stopped moving, James." Tristan raised

a mocking eyebrow as he unzipped his jeans and exposed the enormous erection stretching his boxers.

James gulped and hastily got rid of his pants and underwear.

Tristan studied his body with a hooded stare that made his nerve endings tingle and his dick ache. "Nice." He flashed a sinful smile at James, pushed down the last items of clothing covering his incredible physique, and stepped out of them.

James's gaze locked on Tristan's cock. His mouth watered. *Fuck.*

It was meaty and long, just like he'd fantasized it would be. And right now, it was swollen and hard for him, the veins covering the silken, flushed skin full and throbbing.

"James?"

"What?" James mumbled distractedly.

"Keep the shirt."

Tristan opened the nightstand and fished out a box of condoms and a bottle of lube.

James fingered the top button of his shirt nervously. "You really want me to keep this on?"

"White looks good on you." Tristan brought the condoms and lube over.

James sucked in air when he grabbed his ankle and tugged him closer.

Tristan sat him on the edge of the bed and nudged his knees open.

"Besides, the thought of making a mess of you while you're wearing it really turns me on," he growled, his pupils round with lust. He clasped James's head in his large hands, tilted his face up, and leaned down to ravish his lips.

James moaned and fisted his fingers in the sheets as Tristan worked their tongues in a blistering mating dance. His cock jerked where it jutted proudly from his trimmed pubes, his erection pulsing with every seductive suck of Tristan's mouth.

The first delicious wave of another climax washed through his body.

James shuddered. He wanted Tristan's mouth to bring him to his next orgasm.

Tristan unbuttoned his shirt and spread the material open. James twitched when he danced his fingers lightly down his chest and abs. His belly spasmed under Tristan's touch as he followed his treasure trail.

Tristan grazed his shaft with his knuckles.

"*Fuck!*" James closed his eyes and jerked, his hips rolling instinctively into Tristan's touch.

"Not yet." Tristan knelt between James's legs and spread his thighs wide open, his expression tight. "There's a lot more I want to do to you before I sink my cock inside your body."

Before James could process that sinful image, Tristan leaned down and sucked the tip of his shaft inside his mouth.

Pleasure had James crying out and his body jackknifing off the bed. The motion shoved his erection all the way to the back of Tristan's throat. Tristan grunted around his flesh.

The way he kneaded James's thighs with his hands told him he didn't mind.

James hissed, head tilting and eyes almost rolling back inside his skull at the filthy feeling. He'd never deep-throated a man before.

His cock felt like it was trapped inside a tight, hot velvet tunnel.

James's breath locked in his lungs when he looked down and met Tristan's scalding gaze. Tristan slowly pulled off his dick, his cheeks hollowing in a powerful sucking motion that made James see stars.

"Oh God!" James whimpered. "I'm gonna—*I'm gonna come!*"

Tristan let go of James's cock with a wet pop that made his ass contract. He pinned him with a sultry stare and closed his fingers tightly around the base of James's shaft.

James startled, an incoherent sound leaving him at the pleasure pain.

"No, you won't." Tristan straightened and kissed him. "I'm going to eat you to my heart's content before that happens."

James moaned when he tasted himself on Tristan's tongue.

Then Tristan lowered his head and kept his promise, his grip locked punishingly on the root of James's cock while he licked, sucked, and teased his shaft and tip with his wicked tongue and lips.

A sob escaped James when Tristan swallowed him inside the silken depths of his throat and bobbed his head slow and deep. He experienced his first dry orgasm within minutes, one hand sinking in Tristan's hair while he grasped the sheets with the other and danced wildly inside Tristan's mouth.

Tristan didn't let go until James collapsed on his back in a quivering, sweaty mess, his entire being quaking from his third dry climax. He moaned when Tristan loosened his tight hold on his dick.

His cock felt like it would explode at the slightest touch.

James's chest shuddered with his labored breathing as he pushed up on his elbows and looked down the length of his body to meet Tristan's dark gaze where he knelt between his legs.

"Come for me," Tristan said huskily.

He flicked the tip of James's cock with his tongue, took him inside his mouth, and sucked once.

James's body bowed off the bed. Blood roared in his skull and his vision flickered when his orgasm crashed over him. He was barely aware of his guttural shouts as he bent his knees, pressed his heels on the edge of the bed, and ejaculated violently inside Tristan's mouth, his hips thrusting jerkily while a pleasure so fierce it was almost pain seared his senses.

It was a while before his awareness returned.

James panted heavily and blinked, his face and body soaked with sweat.

Tristan had maneuvered him into the middle of the bed and was leaning over him on all fours.

"Your O face is amazing," he groaned.

James flushed.

Fire burned in Tristan's hooded eyes as he lowered

his head and kissed him with a bone deep hunger. "I can't wait to see you like that when I'm deep inside you."

James trembled when Tristan dipped a hand in the shadowy space under his balls and grazed his pucker.

Tristan took James's wrists, stretched his arms above his head, and lowered his body to the bed. They both groaned when their flesh made contact, chest to chest and groin to aching groin.

Tristan's erection probed James's thigh.

"I want to touch you," James breathed, heart pounding.

"Later." Tristan nipped at his lower lip. "I'll go off like a bomb if you put your hand on my dick right now. And the first place I intend to come tonight is inside your ass."

James nearly swallowed his tongue.

All rational thought left his mind as Tristan took his time exploring his body, his fingers, lips, and tongue wreaking the sweetest havoc on James's senses. Tristan caressed, kneaded, kissed, and licked every inch of skin he came across, the low growls rumbling from his chest sending delicious shivers down James's spine while his stubble scratched James's skin and made his nerve endings tingle.

He played with James's nipples and grinned at the way he hissed and bucked his hips when he twisted the hard nubs.

"I see you like a bit of pain with your pleasure," he teased.

James tried to answer. His words turned into an

incoherent garble when Tristan closed his teeth on his left nipple and tugged. His erection throbbed and pulsed out precum over their bellies.

Tristan groaned. "Jesus, I love your scent." He slipped a hand between their bodies and captured a drop leaking from the tip.

James shuddered at his touch.

"It tastes pretty damn good too." Tristan grinned wickedly before licking his finger and moving up to kiss James.

James moaned and clutched Tristan's head when he tasted himself on his tongue. "Fuck! I want you inside me!"

CHAPTER ELEVEN

TRISTAN'S EYES BLAZED. "I HAVE TO GET YOU READY first. I'm pretty big."

He took James's hand and guided his fingers to his erection.

James shivered at his size. He tugged gently on Tristan's shaft. "Hurry."

Tristan groaned and closed his eyes for a second, fighting for control. He grabbed the lube, snaked down the bed, and spread James's legs open. James's belly tightened as Tristan knelt in the cradle of his body and hooked his knees around his hips. Their gazes stayed locked as he opened the bottle and poured out a generous amount of lube in his hand.

James reached up and ran his fingers lightly across Tristan's chest and the mesmerizing swirls of his tattoos, unable to keep still. The way Tristan sucked in air and his muscles contracted beneath his touch told him he liked what he was doing.

James took this as a sign of approval and explored

Tristan's rock hard six-pack and abs to his heart's content while Tristan warmed the lube between his palms.

Then Tristan pushed his right thigh up and touched his ass.

James's breath stuttered at the sinful sensation. He couldn't help arching his back as Tristan circled his pucker with the pads of his slick fingers. He moaned, the folds guarding his entrance tingling and twitching as Tristan rubbed and teased them.

Tristan waited until his opening softened before pushing a finger inside him.

"*Oh!*" James bit his lip, his ass clenching around the intruder.

Tristan kissed his inner thigh. "You like that?"

James nodded jerkily, sweat beading his face.

Tristan started thrusting in and out of James's body, his expression focused. James hummed and squeezed his hole, enjoying the sinful feeling.

Tristan pushed a second finger inside him and scissored his digits.

James tensed at the stinging. Tristan's fingers were much thicker than his own.

"You're pretty tight," Tristan grunted.

James swallowed as he met Tristan's tense gaze. He wasn't about to admit that, beside the sex toys he'd used to try and stimulate himself to an orgasm, he was the first man he would be allowing inside his body in a number of years.

"It's—been a while," he confessed.

Tristan clenched his jaw, eyes narrowing a little.

"Somehow, I get the feeling there's more to unpack there, but I don't think I can't stop right now," he said in a voice thick with desire. He hooked his fingers a little.

James gasped at the wicked sensation. "I don't want you to stop."

Tristan grunted and resumed thrusting his fingers. He grabbed the lube, poured some of it directly on James's twitching opening, and worked his passage briskly.

James grasped the pillow under his head and clenched his jaw when Tristan inserted a third finger inside him.

Tristan paused. "Does it hurt?"

James licked his lips and met his strained stare. "A little. But I can bear it."

Tristan grimaced. "I'm bigger than three fingers." He looked at his erection.

James followed his gaze. He couldn't deny the wariness that darted through him as he studied Tristan's thick girth in a fresh light.

But he also wanted this. He wanted Tristan inside him more than he'd ever wanted anything in his life.

A rueful sigh left Tristan as he observed James's expression. "I'll try to go slow." He slipped his fingers out of James, ripped open a condom, and sheathed himself.

James's pulse raced as he watched Tristan lube up.

This was the moment of truth. Would he be able to experience pleasure with another's man cock inside his ass?

He hadn't the last few times he'd had anal sex.

But then again, this was Tristan.

James's breath stuttered with a mix of alarm and excitement when Tristan spread his thighs nice and wide, and pressed the head of his cock to his hole.

"Breathe, James."

James did just that as Tristan slowly pushed in.

Tristan's dick breached his opening. He nudged his hips forward.

"*Fuck!*" James dug his fingers in Tristan's thighs and shuddered.

His ass felt like it was about to tear.

Tristan leaned down and kissed him. "Relax, James." He touched James's cock.

"Oh!" James shivered, his lower body throbbing at the dual stimulation.

Pleasure gradually overcame pain as Tristan stroked him with a featherlight touch.

Tristan rolled his hips and entered his body another inch.

James winced at the fierce burning that erupted deep inside his hole. "Shit!"

His stomach curdled. He stared blindly at Tristan, frozen by fear.

Tristan's expression softened. "I'm here." He kissed James with a gentleness that made his heart ache. "I've got you." He nuzzled his nose. "I'll stop if you want me to."

James swallowed heavily. He shook his head.

Tristan kept his hips still, poured more lube in his

hand, and started rubbing James's slicked up cock briskly, the tightness in his face telling its own story.

James closed his eyes, aware Tristan's rigid self-control was the only thing stopping him from penetrating him fully. Relief shuddered through him.

Thank God I'm still hard!

Goosebumps broke out across his skin as Tristan pleasured him. A delicious tingling spread through his stomach and spine at Tristan's expert touch. To his surprise, his passage slowly relaxed as his body adapted to Tristan's girth.

Tristan circled the tip of his aching dick with a teasing thumb. James moaned. A gasp left him when Tristan pressed his fingers firmly against his quivering taint.

Tristan smiled at his dazed expression and leaned down to nibble on his ear. "This will make you come faster." He kept pushing against the taut skin under James's balls while he increased the motion of his hand on James's cock.

Pleasure rapidly knotted James's belly. It throbbed and expanded with every sinful stroke of Tristan's fingers and the insistent pressure against his taint.

His orgasm took him by surprise and wrenched a shocked cry from his lips.

James's eyes rounded as his passage convulsed and opened around the solid cock inside him, his ejaculation so forceful cum splashed up his chest as he gasped and groaned.

Tristan gritted his teeth, pushed through the tight

ring of inner muscles protecting his insides and punched home with a deep stroke of his hips.

James shuddered as Tristan finally bottomed out inside him, his body still twitching and his cock oozing. The sharp sting of Tristan's penetration was overshadowed by the incredible pleasure still sparking his senses and the thrill of having his ass stuffed to the brim.

He didn't realize he'd scored scratches in Tristan's thighs until he came down from his high and his vision focused.

"Sorry." he mumbled, hastily letting go.

Tristan lifted his hand and kissed his palm, his eyes dark with desire. "Don't be. I like that you've marked me."

James shivered at his hungry expression, his chest tightening with more than just desire. "Tristan?"

"Yeah?"

James squeezed his hole tentatively. Tristan swore.

"Fuck me," James breathed.

A feral sound left Tristan.

His sweat splashed hotly on James's chest as he grasped his hip, pressed a hand on the sheets by his head, and leaned forward. The new angle tilted James's body at a delicious angle that drew throaty hisses from them both and had Tristan sinking even deeper inside him.

Tristan bowed his body, pulled back, and pushed back in.

James's breath stuttered at the carnal sensation, the last of his pain fading ahead of a heat and fullness he had never known before. This was different from all the times he'd ever had a man inside him.

Sex with Tristan was…perfection.

They gasped and groaned as they fell under a sensual spell, James's hips rising and falling to meet Tristan's delicious trusts in a dance as old as time. He clenched Tristan's thick cock tightly with his passage and was rewarded with an animal sound.

"I'm gonna lose my mind if you do that!" Tristan growled.

James caressed his face and leaned up to bite his jawline. "Maybe I want you to lose your mind."

Tristan closed his eyes and shuddered. Then he kissed James like he needed him for air, pushed his thighs even wider, and gave in to his body's instincts.

James's heart thundered violently against his ribs as Tristan took him like he wanted to, powerful hips punching his cock in and out of him. James reached down and started stroking himself as his body accepted everything Tristan had to give. He shivered, stunned by how much more sensitive and receptive his flesh had become.

He owed it to the man claiming him with a passionate strength born of pure desire.

Tristan grunted as he chased his pleasure, his face tightening.

A hot, sweet ache built deep inside James as his motions accelerated. Then Tristan pressed his thighs to his chest and hit a spot inside him that made James see stars.

"*Oh!*" James's eyes rounded at the hot bolt that had just speared his lower body and ass. "Is that—?!"

"Yeah, that's your prostate." Tristan gnashed his teeth and hit that spot over and over again as he thrust inside James.

Blinding pleasure overtook James. He twisted his hands in the sheets by his head and cried out as an ecstasy he had never known swept over him like a storm. He heard Tristan chant his name above the dull roar of blood in his skull as he ejaculated fiercely, the violent convulsions shaking his body causing his ass to clench rhythmically.

His spasms finally tipped Tristan over the edge.

James blinked sweat out of his eyes when Tristan let out an animal sound and went rigid above him. His breath locked in his throat.

Tristan's face flushed a ruddy red and the muscles in his neck corded as he climaxed. Feral grunts escaped his clenched teeth. His fingers sank painfully in James's thighs when he started moving again, his hips jackknifing his cock erratically in and out of James's ass, his glazed eyes locked on the place where their bodies merged.

It was a while before he shuddered to a stop and took a ragged breath, his body quaking with aftershocks of pleasure. Sweat oozed down his brow and face and landed hotly on James's belly.

Tristan raised his head and finally met James's gaze.

"That was unreal," he said huskily.

James's pulse thrummed a rapid tempo in his veins as he nodded shakily, too spent to even speak. He shivered when Tristan trailed a finger through the cum painting his stomach.

"You came a lot."

James's cock twitched at the banked heat in Tristan's eyes. Tristan slowly pulled out of his body. James bit his lip and moaned at the way his insides clung hungrily to his cock.

Tristan peeled the used condom off.

James blinked. "Oh."

Tristan was still semi-erect.

They both eyed the box of condoms on the sheets.

"How sore are you?" Tristan asked in a tone full of hope.

James swallowed. "Not that sore."

Truth be told, he could still feel Tristan's thick shape inside him.

But he very much wanted to experience what they'd just done all over again, even it meant he might not be able to walk in the morning.

Tristan pursed his lips. "You'll regret that statement tomorrow."

"I'll take a hot bath before I leave."

Tristan chuckled at the fervent promise. He leaned down and kissed James. "My, my, someone really wants my dick inside him."

James tugged Tristan's lower lip between his teeth and reached between their bodies to grasp his swelling cock. "Stop talking and put this where it belongs, Mr. Hart."

Tristan's eyes blazed at the throaty command. "Yes, sir."

CHAPTER TWELVE

THE SHRILL CALL OF A SCRUB JAY ROUSED TRISTAN THE next morning. He blinked, rolled onto his back, and stretched out a hand beside him.

The sheets were lukewarm and empty.

He sat up and looked around the room, his grogginess vanishing. A sliver of pale light framed the edge of the curtains.

It was barely dawn.

He could tell from the silence in the cabin that he was alone.

Tristan frowned and rubbed a hand down his face.

He and James hadn't exactly made any promises beyond last night. But then again, they'd hardly spoken aside from that poignant moment on his porch.

Nope, we just fucked a lot.

Vivid memories danced across his inner vision, stirring his dick.

Sex with James had been as incredible as he'd imagined it would be. And he'd been right. Behind the icy composure James usually displayed was a passionate and very much hedonistic soul.

Tristan could still hear the wild sounds James had made while he'd been inside him. To say that they'd turned him on like little else could, would be an understatement. He suspected making James shout out in pleasure was something he could get addicted to real fast.

They'd had sex another three times before sleep had finally claimed them.

Tristan sighed. He'd discovered belatedly that James had a particular fetish about being tied up and taken from behind. Fucking him while he'd knelt and clung to the bed frame with his shirt trapping his wrists had been one insane ride he wouldn't have minded repeating this morning.

He found James's note taped to his refrigerator.

It said *'Call me'* next to his number.

A soft smile curved Tristan's mouth. Despite the curtness of the message, he was willing to bet a hundred bucks it had taken all of James's courage to write it. He folded the note and tucked it in the pocket of his jeans.

It was the start of the weekend tomorrow. He'd give James a call tonight and ask him if he wanted to come over. Or he could go to L.A. and see him. Of course, he needed to find out where he lived first.

Tristan went about his day, his mind full of the man who'd bewitched him.

He hadn't had time to ask him what he'd meant last night, when he'd said he hadn't sex in a while. James was incredibly sensual once his barriers were down and he seemed like the kind of guy who'd have a healthy sexual appetite.

All of Tristan's best laid plans about meeting up with James went awry when Izzy called him at his garage later that morning.

Miles Martinez had woken up.

JAMES CHECKED HIS PHONE FOR WHAT FELT LIKE THE hundredth time.

It was Friday night and Tristan still hadn't called.

After going through all kinds of crazy scenarios like his note falling under Tristan's refrigerator or being blown into the lake by some freak wind, James was coming to the bleak realization that Wednesday night might not have been as special for Tristan as it had been for him.

"Hey, you okay?"

James looked up at the man cooking up a storm in the state of the art kitchen he sat in.

Hugo Strong, Crazyknot's bass player, was making dinner.

The low rumble of voices came from the lounge where the rest of the band was chilling.

James tucked his cell away and rolled the neck of his beer bottle between his fingers, determined not to let his disappointment overshadow their evening. "Yeah. It's...been a long week."

"This is the first time in a while that we've had a

free weekend," Hugo observed. "You should make the most of it and get some rest."

James swallowed a sigh. He couldn't exactly tell Hugo his plans this weekend had centered around a man he couldn't stop thinking about and his out of this world body.

Not to mention that cock.

Thought it had been over twenty-four hours since Tristan had been inside him, he could still feel the shape of his dick inside his pleasantly aching ass.

Lewis Brandt strolled inside the kitchen and grabbed a soda from Hugo's refrigerator. "Is the food ready? I'm starving."

Kurt Taylor and Robbie Cantrell trooped in after him.

Kurt tapped Lewis lightly on the back of his head as he made for a cabinet and started taking out dishes and cutlery. "How about you show some gratitude for the free meal?"

Lewis pouted. "I offered to show my gratitude with sexual favors, but he kept refusing."

"I heard that." Mia Carroway, Hugo's long term girlfriend, breezed inside the room. "Hi, honey." She dropped a kiss on Hugo's mouth.

"Hey, sweetheart." Hugo's eyes shone warmly as he gave her a quick hug. "How was your day?"

"The children were wilder than usual." Mia grimaced. "I think there's something in the water."

Hugo grinned. He'd met Mia at night school, before Crazyknot rose to notoriety. That had been ten years ago.

Mia ruffled Lewis's hair like he was one of her elementary school kids and stole his soda.

Lewis sucked in air as he watched her take a generous gulp. "Ooh, an indirect kiss!" He looked from Mia to Hugo. "Does that mean you guys would be open to a threesome?"

Kurt rolled his eyes as he finished setting the dining table.

Mia patted Lewis's chest lightly, a veneer of steel underlying her light tone. "That's a nice offer and all, but I don't share. Also, no offense, your confidence might shrink when you see Hugo's dick."

Lewis sucked in air. Hugo snorted, his shoulders trembling.

James hid a smile behind his drink. Mia and Kurt were the only ones who could keep Lewis under control besides him.

"I mean, she's not wrong," Robbie muttered.

"Hey!" Lewis protested. "We've all seen each other's dick at one time or another. How much bigger could his have grown?"

"It's grown plenty," Mia assured.

Hugo rolled his eyes. "Babe."

Mia kissed his cheek. "I know you love it when I talk dirty."

"It's okay, Lou Lou." Robbie grasped Lewis's shoulder and gave him a commiserating look. "You'll go through your growth spurt soon."

Lewis scowled while the rest of them laughed.

Dinner was a lively affair, as it always was. With Crazyknot's schedule usually packed like crazy, they tried to meet up at least a couple of times a month for a get together meal. The only one missing tonight was Roman. The conversation soon turned to Crazyknot's lead singer and the building project he'd taken on.

"Do you think he'll see it through?" Hugo pondered as he and Mia cleared the table.

All eyes turned to James. He ran a hand through his hair and sighed ruefully.

"I hate to admit it but, the place he bought is pretty special."

And the guy doing it up and *doing him is kinda exceptional too.*

Though he'd had his reservations about Drake, James had to admit the man was as solid as a rock when it came to Roman. The way Roman openly trusted him made that doubly clear. James still harbored mixed feelings about losing his role as Roman's protector to Drake, but he knew Drake could give Roman something he couldn't.

"Christ," Kurt muttered. "I never thought I'd see the day Roman settles down in the outback."

Mia raised an eyebrow. "Twilight Falls is hardly the outback, Kurt. The place is one of the top tourist destinations in this part of California."

"You know what I mean though." Kurt grimaced and waved a hand vaguely. "Roman is…city life and rock 'n' roll, not cozy home and fuzzy slippers."

"Who knows?" Hugo said steadily. "Maybe that's all he's ever wanted."

James could guess the words Hugo didn't voice out loud. Roman's childhood being the god awful nightmare it had been, a stable home was probably what he yearned for the most in the world.

His cell vibrated in his pocket, distracting him. He took it out and stiffened when he saw the caller ID.

It was Tristan.

"Sorry, I have to take this." James rose and answered the call as he headed swiftly into the lounge. "Tristan?"

"Hi."

James's pulse quickened at Tristan's gravelly voice. He'd almost forgotten the effect it had on him. The tension knotting his shoulders loosened a fraction.

"I was getting worried you wouldn't call," he said bluntly.

There was a short silence.

Tristan sighed. "I'm sorry, I meant to do that yesterday. It's been a crazy couple of days. But that's not why I'm calling you."

James tensed a little at his grave tone. "What do you mean?"

"You need to come to Twilight Falls."

James blinked. His face warmed up. "I—I can make it later tonight. I'm at a friend's house right now."

"That's not what I meant either." Tristan paused. "Strike that. I very much intended to call you over and spend this weekend fucking you into Monday. Or I was going to go to your place and check out your garage."

James bit his lip. He knew Tristan was thinking about one particular fantasy of his they both yearned to fulfill. Something that felt very much like happiness warmed his belly. Tristan was evidently as keen as he was to resume what they'd started two nights ago.

His next words made James's blood curdle and scattered his feverish imagination.

"You need to come to Twilight Falls because of Roman. His dad turned up on his doorstep tonight and attacked him. I'm at the police station with Roman and Drake right now."

A buzzing sounded in James's ears. He started hyperventilating as his worse fears played out before his vision.

Roman! Oh God! He squeezed his eyes shut and bent over, fighting for air. *Please—please don't tell me he—!*

Someone called his name dimly. It took a moment to make out Tristan's voice.

"James!"

It snapped him out of the panic attack about to overwhelm him.

"Breathe. Roman is okay. He wasn't hurt. Drake turned up and took care of his dad."

Relief made James weak. He clung to the cold marble of the fireplace and dropped on his haunches, his body trembling.

"Thank God!" he whispered shakily. "I thought—I really thought—!"

"I'm sorry." Tristan's tone was full of remorse. "I should have made that clear sooner."

James swallowed convulsively and shook his head. He realized belatedly that Tristan couldn't see him.

"It's okay. Thank you for calling me." He took a shuddering breath. "I'll be there as soon as I can."

Now that his initial shock was subsiding, he couldn't help the dread that sent his heart pounding as the ramifications of what Tristan had told him raced through his mind. He had to stay on top of this before some reporter got wind of the incident.

"Alright," Tristan murmured. "Be careful and drive safely."

James's stomach clenched, grateful for the concern and affection in Tristan's voice. It gave him much needed strength.

"I will." He ended the call and pressed a hand to his face.

"James?" someone said behind him.

He turned. Hugo had come into the room.

The bass player startled when he saw his expression. "What's wrong?"

James straightened, his legs no longer shaky.

"I have to go. Something happened to Roman."

Alarm tightened Hugo's face.

"What happened to Roman?" Kurt had come up behind Hugo, his face similarly tense.

The rest of the band was right behind the guitarist.

James cursed under his breath.

The mutinous look dawning in everyone's eyes made it clear wherever he was going, they were coming too.

CHAPTER THIRTEEN

"I can't believe you beat the crap out of the guy," Tristan told Drake as they came out of the police station. "I'll be surprised if he doesn't press charges."

"He violated the terms of his probation and attacked Roman," Drake growled. "That asshole doesn't have a leg to stand on."

"Is your hand okay?" Roman asked Drake anxiously.

The anger knotting Drake's shoulders visibly drained out of him. "It's nothing time won't heal."

Tristan studied the couple shrewdly out the corner of his eyes.

Yup, they're definitely fucking.

Drake and Roman had just finished giving their statements to a couple of Twilight Falls police officers. Excitement had gripped the station when the men and women who worked there realized Crazyknot's lead singer had been involved in the assault reported to 911 earlier that evening. Twilight Falls didn't exactly have a high crime rate and a juicy incident centered around a world famous rockstar had grasped their attention like little else could.

Luckily, the sheriff had gotten on top of his officers' rabid curiosity with a few stern words about what he would personally do to them if he found out they'd blabbed to the press about the disturbance at the Strickland Estate.

Tristan's lips quirked.

Old man Coulton hasn't changed much in the last twenty years.

Gary Coulton had been the sheriff when Tristan and his friends started earning their reputation as the Terrible Seven. Though he'd been hard on them, he'd also been fair and had never held a grudge, even that one time they spray painted his patrol car a vicious purple.

Tristan furrowed his brow a little as he glanced at Drake's swollen knuckles. It wasn't often one of them got into a fist fight these days.

It showed exactly how much Drake cared for Roman.

"You should ice that when you get home."

"We will," Roman blurted out before Drake could answer. He bit his lip.

Tristan's thoughtful gaze swung from Roman to Drake. "So, there *is* something going on between you."

Roman raised his chin defiantly. He startled when Drake twisted on his heels and embraced him tightly. "Drake?" he mumbled, alarmed.

Drake shuddered. "I'm sorry I wasn't there for you." He pulled back and studied Roman with a tortured expression, a muscle jumping in his jawline. "That bastard almost—"

"Don't." Roman shook his head shakily. "You were there for me, Drake. Just like you've been there for me these past few days." He rose on his tip toes and brushed his lips across Drake's mouth, heedless of Tristan watching them. "You gave me the strength I needed to stand up to my father."

Drake's eyes darkened with emotion. He took Roman's right hand and kissed his palm. "That was all you. You were amazing."

Color flooded Roman's face. "James had us take self-defense classes a few years ago. I just made sure to keep to an open space and use whatever I could find around me as a weapon."

This earned Tristan's respect even more. Though Roman came across as fragile, he'd managed to fight off his attacker, a man who had clearly terrorized him in the past. Not for the first time, Tristan wondered at the dark secrets Roman and James had harbored over the years of their friendship.

"Still, you were incredibly brave to stand up to him." Drake kissed Roman lightly.

"You guys realize we're still in a public parking lot, right?" Tristan drawled.

Roman glanced guiltily at the brightly-lit building behind them.

Drake squinted at Tristan. "Remind me again why I called you?"

"Cause I'm the only one of your friends not actively

in a relationship right now and, ergo, not having sex," Tristan said gruffly.

This was a lie, but Drake didn't need to know that.

Tristan drove the couple to Drake's home at Roman's insistence. His pulse quickened when a silver Jaguar appeared in the headlights of his pickup as he neared the end of Drake's driveway.

A Porsche he didn't recognize was parked next to it.

Roman stared. "What are they doing there?"

"I called James when I was at the station," Tristan said evasively.

Roman narrowed his eyes at Tristan's reflection in the rearview mirror. "How come you have James's number?"

Tristan shrugged. "I fixed his car when he came to Twilight Falls last week."

Drake gave Tristan a shrewd look.

"Great." Roman sighed as he watched the men pouring out of the two vehicles. "The whole gang's here."

⁂

JAMES'S HEART POUNDED WHEN ROMAN STEPPED OUT OF Tristan's pickup. He rushed over and hugged him, the fear humming through him ebbing away with a suddenness that left him weak.

"Thank God you're okay!"

Roman rocked back on his heels before squeezing his arms tightly around James. "Yeah," he mumbled against his shoulder.

The way he trembled told James he hadn't completely gotten over the shock of what had happened to him. He reluctantly let go of Roman when the rest of Crazyknot crowded noisily around them and took turns hugging Roman while they voiced their relief. His gaze found Tristan.

"You okay?" Tristan mouthed.

James dipped his chin lightly, the ice filling his veins melting under Tristan's stare.

"We should go in," Drake said.

Kurt and Hugo measured him carefully with their gazes. James had told them about Drake while they'd been waiting outside the guy's home.

Lewis's eyes gleamed with interest as he scanned Drake. He leaned toward Robbie. "That guy's hot," he said in a stage whisper out of the corner of his mouth.

"Yeah, I think they're fucking," Robbie mumbled, looking from Drake to Roman and back.

James swallowed a groan.

Robbie could be terribly astute despite his devil-may-care attitude.

All of Crazyknot studied Roman expectantly.

Roman scowled when Lewis opened his mouth. "Not one more word out of you! We are *not* talking about this out here. Inside, right now!" He indicated Drake's home with a commanding finger.

"Alright, Princess," Lewis grumbled.

"Jeez, keep your panties on," Robbie muttered.

James lingered at the back as they trooped inside the house.

A warm hand grasped his wrist and pulled him into

the shadows of Drake's porch. The door closed softly behind Kurt.

James's mouth went dry when he found himself trapped between Tristan and the wall of Drake's home.

"Hey." Tristan nuzzled his nose and pressed a light kiss to his mouth, his eyes gleaming in the gloom.

Desire singed through James's veins. He pressed his body closer, grasped Tristan's face, and deepened the kiss.

By the time their lips parted, they were both breathing hard.

"Hi," James managed in a strangled voice.

Tristan smiled. "I like that I do that to you."

James's gaze focused on Tristan's lips. He wanted them on his mouth again.

"Do what?" he said distractedly.

"That I make you hot and flustered."

Heat flooded James's face. He couldn't exactly deny this.

Tristan's low laugh danced down his spine and raised goosebumps on his skin.

He took James's hand and kissed his knuckles. "I missed you."

Emotion clogged James's throat at the sincere words. "I missed you too."

Tristan took him in his arms and quietly embraced him. "Let's just stay like this for a minute," he murmured with a soft sigh. "I need to recharge."

James swallowed and relaxed. A peaceful feeling settled over him as he listened to the strong beat of Tristan's heart.

He knew they needed to talk about what was happening between them. They'd gone about things completely the wrong way. They'd kissed the first day they'd met and had sex the second time they'd found themselves in each other's company.

Both were out of character for James and he suspected it was the same for Tristan.

"The reason I didn't call you yesterday was because Miles woke up," Tristan murmured in his hair.

James startled. He drew back and stared at Tristan, stunned. "He woke up?!"

He'd learned about the seventh member of the Terrible Seven from Carter. The chances of Miles Martinez ever opening his eyes again had been one in a million.

"Yeah." Tristan shuddered. "We were all pretty shook up. We spent most of yesterday and today at the care home." He swallowed convulsively. "Having him back is an honest to God miracle."

James squeezed his arms around Tristan. He could tell he carried the same guilt he'd seen in Carter's eyes when the movie star had spoken about Miles.

It looks like this week has been a whirlwind for both of us, in more ways than one.

"Is he gonna be okay?"

"I think so. He had a check-up at the hospital and they seemed pretty happy with him. They think he'll be able to come home by the end of the month."

James smiled. "That's great."

Tristan pursed his lips and hugged him close. "I meant what I said on the phone. I had major plans this weekend and they all involved being naked with you."

James chuckled at his aggrieved tone. Tristan's honesty was as refreshing as it was unexpected. It made his heart tingle with happiness.

He was falling for the man and no one was more surprised by that than him.

Tristan finally pulled back and gazed somberly into James's eyes. "This thing with Roman. It's not gonna blow over overnight, is it?"

James hesitated. "I don't know yet. But I need to be ready for every eventuality." He clenched his jaw. "That asshole might have talked to the press already."

Tristan grimaced. "You mean Roman's father?"

James nodded.

"About that." Tristan lifted a hand and grazed James's cheek lightly with a knuckle, concern darkening his eyes. "You'll find this out soon enough, but I'd rather be the one to tell you. He followed you, that Wednesday night."

James blinked, not sure he'd heard right. "What?"

A muscle jumped in Tristan's cheek. "It's not your fault, James. The cops reckoned he'd been stalking you for a week."

Horror squeezed James's heart as he finally grasped Tristan's meaning.

The reason Dusty Leyman had found Roman and attacked him tonight was because of him.

A tortured sound escaped James.

Tristan swore and took him in his arms again as he started to shake.

"Don't do this to yourself. He would have found Roman eventually. Better that Drake was there tonight to stop him."

James shuddered and clung to Tristan, grateful for his quiet strength. His breath choked as the rollercoaster of emotions he'd gone through that evening finally gave way to tears.

Tristan sighed ruefully. "You'll steam up your glasses if you do that." He took James's specs off and studied him as he sniveled and wiped his nose with the back of his hand.

"James?"

"Yeah?"

"I hate to say this, but you're kinda an ugly crier," Tristan stated solemnly.

James sucked in air, his tears stopping as abruptly as they'd started.

Tristan chuckled and let out a fake "*Ouch!*" when he punched him in the chest.

CHAPTER FOURTEEN

"Fuck. Me," Izzy mumbled. "It's Crazyknot and their hot, brooding manager."

James squinted at the brunette as he approached her table, Roman, Drake, and the rest of Crazyknot at his heels. "I'm not sure if that's a compliment or an insult."

Izzy smiled impishly.

James greeted Wyatt and Nathan and introduced the other members of Crazyknot.

It was Saturday night and Drake had brought them to *The Watering Hole,* the only gay bar in Twilight Falls and this part of the San Bernardino Mountains. Though James had had his reservations when Roman had mentioned the place that afternoon, the others had soon convinced him they needed the distraction.

It had been a turbulent twenty-four hours. After the incident that had led to Roman's father's arrest, they'd talked late into the night at Drake's place before bedding down in his guest bedrooms and in the lounge.

Roman and Drake had spent most of Saturday

afternoon showing Crazyknot around the Strickland Estate while James had a conference call with Roman's lawyers concerning the attack. To his relief, they'd assured him Roman's father would soon be back behind bars for an indefinite period.

Roman had sagged with relief when James had told him that piece of news.

Izzy introduced Sam Harris and Imogen Hart presently.

Hunter's manager at *Go Thomson!* studied Kurt and the others with a glazed look before leaning sideways toward Sam. "Am I dreaming?" she mumbled. "I'm dreaming, right?"

"Nope, it's really them." Elijah's bakery manager raked the members of Crazyknot with her gaze like she was committing their measurements to memory.

Lewis grinned at Izzy. "About what you said. It would be rude to partake in sexual intercourse in public. Although, this place looks like it has a back room, so why don't we take a walk and—*Ouch!*"

James rolled his eyes as both Roman and Kurt stepped on Lewis's feet.

Wyatt frowned.

"Have I told you lately that the two of you are serious cock blockers?" Lewis grumbled.

"Izzy is off limits," Roman said. "And, FYI, the guy sitting next to her looking like he's about to stab you is her brother."

Izzy ignored her scowling sibling and smiled sweetly at Roman. "Oh, how nice of you to defend me." She arched an eyebrow at Lewis. "I don't mind taking this little kid for a ride. Who knows, he might even learn some new tricks."

"K-kid?!" Lewis spluttered.

Kurt and the others smirked.

"I'm gonna buy you a drink just for that," James told Izzy.

"You seen the other guys?" Drake asked as they pulled the next table and chairs over.

"Alex and Finn said they were gonna drop by the care home first. The rest of them should be here soon." Movement near the door drew Izzy's attention. "Speak of the devil."

James's heartbeat accelerated.

Carter, Elijah, Hunter, and Theo were heading their way. Tristan was with them.

Imogen's eyes glazed over. "I think my ovaries just exploded."

James swallowed, his dick twitching. *You and me both.*

Tristan in black jeans and a leather jacket looked like a present he very much wanted to unwrap.

❧

THE EXCITED BUZZ FILLING *THE WATERING HOLE* WAS Tristan's first hint that something was going on. His belly contracted when he scanned the interior and spotted James and Crazyknot sitting with Izzy and the others.

"What the hell are they doing here?" Carter muttered as they made their way across the bar.

"Looks like you have competition," Hunter told him with a grin.

Carter rolled his eyes.

Tristan nodded a greeting at the other members of Crazyknot while Roman made introductions. He sat across from James and met his gaze.

The slight flush reddening James's ears and the way he licked his lips told Tristan he was as hyperaware of Tristan as he was of him. Alas, neither of them could do anything about the electricity sparking between them, especially after a queue of autograph seekers formed at their table.

"Ten bucks says this is going to be all over tomorrow's local papers," Nathan drawled when the last of them left.

"It's already on social media." Sam was scrolling through her phone.

"How come they aren't asking you for your autograph?" Hugo asked Carter curiously.

Carter grimaced. "You forget I grew up here. Besides, half these people saw me run naked down Main Street when I was ten."

Elijah's eyes rounded. "You ran naked down Main Street?!"

Tristan smiled in his beer as he recalled the incident. They'd stood outside Hunter's dad's hardware store and spurred Carter on.

Carter shrugged. "I lost a bet to Hunter."

Hunter grinned. "I still can't believe you couldn't get a kiss out of Daisy Dickson."

Carter narrowed his eyes. "Yeah, well, not everyone is sensitive to my charms."

"Daisy Dickson is gay," Sam said bluntly.

Shocked inhales erupted around the tables.

"No way." Hunter stared. "But—she went out with half the guys on the baseball team in high school!"

Sam shrugged. "Well, she evidently decided dicks weren't her thing."

Carter turned an inquisitive eye on Hugo and the rest of Crazyknot. "What brings you guys here, anyway? This place is not your normal Saturday night scene."

James and Roman stiffened a little.

Drake shared a guarded look with Tristan.

"We missed Roman, so we decided to visit," Kurt said lightly.

Tristan took a leisurely swig of his drink. "So, have you seen the place Roman bought?"

Drake flashed him a grateful look for steering the conversation in a safe direction. Alex and Finn turned up, adding to the distraction.

Tristan watched as James excused himself and disappeared in the direction of the restroom a short while later. He waited a couple of minutes before slipping away into the crowd.

James was washing his hands when Tristan entered the restroom. His eyes widened in the reflection in the mirror. Tristan looked around.

Two of the cubicles were occupied.

He waited until James hastily dried his hands before

taking him by the wrist and guiding him silently out of the restroom.

"Where—where are we going?" James asked in a breathless voice in the corridor outside.

Tristan flashed him a heated look. "Somewhere no one will see us."

James flushed, his body almost vibrating with excitement.

Tristan exited the bar through a back door, skirted the building to the parking lot at the side, and hustled James inside the back of his pickup. For once, he was grateful he'd found a space away from the streetlights.

James stared at Tristan across the space separating them, his pupils dilated with desire.

They came together in a clash of mouths and grasping hands.

Tristan removed James's glasses and tossed them on the front seat before grabbing his ass and pulling him close.

"God, I've missed this!" James groaned in between their desperate kisses.

"Me too." Tristan nudged his chin up and went to town on his throat.

James tipped his head back on a delicious moan. He kneaded the muscles of Tristan's back and clung to him like he never wanted to let go.

Tristan's erection pressed heavily against his jeans as he savored the salty sweetness of James's skin. He groaned when he smelled the musky scent of his arousal. All he wanted to do right now was strip James of his clothes and sink his cock inside his body until neither of them could move.

He decided to settle for the next best thing.

James gasped when Tristan maneuvered him onto his lap. The color staining his cheekbones deepened as Tristan swiftly unbuckled their pants and freed their erections. He looked down as Tristan grasped their shafts in one large hand, his breathing accelerating when he grasped his intention.

They hissed and shuddered as Tristan started stroking them.

Tristan's heart pounded so fiercely he was surprised James couldn't hear it. The same heady thrill coursing through him was evident in James's bright gaze and dilated pupils. Tristan took his mouth in a scorching kiss as he started rolling his hips deliciously into his touch.

"Have I told you how much I like your eyes?" He nipped at James's lips. "They turn the most beautiful sea green when you're aroused."

James flushed and panted, his fingers digging into Tristan's shoulders.

Tristan pressed a reverent kiss to the hollow of his throat as their dicks throbbed in his grasp. "Every inch of you is exquisite," he breathed.

A lustful sound tumbled out of James's mouth, the frantic way he started moving against Tristan telling him he was close to coming.

Tristan licked and sucked the pulse beating wildly at the base of James's neck as they both chased their pleasure. He grabbed a tissue from his jeans and covered their cocks when they exploded, their passionate grunts echoing hotly in the space between them.

They both relaxed as they slowly came down from their high.

"I could get addicted to your scent," Tristan groaned. He dropped a head against James's shoulder while they shivered and twitched against one another. "Are you going back to L.A. tonight?"

James squeezed his arms around his shoulders and nodded. "Yeah," he murmured reluctantly. "I need to be there in case this thing blows up in our faces."

Tristan sighed. "Well, at least we got something else to blow up tonight." He looked down at their spent dicks.

James laughed. "I like it when you talk dirty." He pressed a sweet kiss to Tristan's mouth and chuckled when Tristan chased after his lips. "I'll call you when things settle down."

"Okay."

CHAPTER FIFTEEN

The scandal about Roman's father broke out early Sunday morning. By the time James called Roman at dawn, it was all over the six a.m. entertainment news. Not only had someone leaked the story to the press, there was a blurry snapshot of Roman and Drake kissing in the parking lot of the police station already circulating on the internet.

James had cursed silently when he'd seen the picture on an infamous paparazzi site.

"James, Drake's with me," Roman said stiffly. "I'm gonna put you on speaker."

James heard Drake murmur something and end his phone conversation with Izzy.

One of her reporter friends had called her that morning and quizzed her about the incident involving Roman. She'd contacted Drake at the same time James had called Roman.

"I'd love to say I didn't foresee this, but I can't," James told the two men without preamble. He paused, remorse shooting through him. "Drake, I'm sorry. The next couple of weeks are gonna be hell for you. Roman is used to the shit storm coming his way, although this is by far the worst scandal he's ever been involved in as a member of Crazyknot."

Sheets rustled at the other end of the line.

"Just tell me what I need to do, James," Drake said. "I'm not exactly a stranger to scandals. I saw what happened to Carter and Elijah when they first got together."

James pursed his lips. This could easily damage Drake's hard-earned reputation and his business. The fact that he still intended to support Roman despite this made James respect the man even more.

Tristan's friends are all commendable.

"Okay, here's how we're gonna play this."

The rest of that day passed in a blur as James got together with the PR department of Crazyknot's agency to put together an official statement on the incident. The court order concerning Roman's past still stood. As such, no one could reveal the finer details of what had happened to the rockstar as a child unless he chose to divulge it himself, or someone interviewed his father. Of course, some of the information concerning Dusty Leyman was in the public domain and the records of his criminal activities were already pasted all over the news.

Thoughts of Tristan drifted through James's mind at various parts of the day as he and the PR team engaged in damage limitation.

He really wanted to continue what they'd started in his pickup yesterday.

Alas, James knew the chances of that happening anytime soon were slim at best. This thing with Roman was going to consume his time and energy for the better part of the coming week.

He ran the press release by Roman before he revealed it at the last minute conference the agency had called that afternoon. Despite the short notice, the room was packed and James found himself under the glare of dozens of cameras and microphones.

He took a shallow breath as he studied the sea of faces before him, the forbidding mask that had earned him the title Ice Princess on full display. It wasn't his first time doing this. Yet, he couldn't help the butterflies in his stomach.

This was personal and he had to make sure he got it right the first time.

"Before I begin, I need to make it clear I won't be taking any questions."

Protests broke out.

"Oh, come on!" a reporter groaned in the front row.

"Zip it, Tom," James snapped.

"Alright, alright, Princess Lang," the guy grumbled.

This earned him chuckles.

James narrowed his eyes. The reporter shut his mouth, as did the rest of the room.

James kept his tone steady as he read from the press release in his hands.

By the time the six p.m. entertainment news went live, the recording was all over the internet.

The official story they'd decided to go with was that Roman came from a background of domestic violence and crime and was forced into an orphanage at age sixteen for his own protection from his father. This provided the hungry press with the perfect backdrop to Roman's addiction problems and his wild behavior in the early stages of his career, including his spectacular fall from grace before he went into rehab a few years ago.

The cynic in James wasn't remotely shocked when sales of Crazyknot's albums soared in the aftermath of the press conference. Everyone loved a sob story and the fact that Roman was the result of the kind of tortured childhood that was all too common in their society these days made the public and big-name celebrities come out in full support of the rockstar.

Drake's role in the event leading to Dusty Leyman's arrest proved to be another point of intense fascination. Roman had come out as gay years ago but had never been seriously romantically linked with anyone. That he'd kissed the man who'd come to his rescue was fodder the gossip channels couldn't get enough of.

James had deliberately not named Drake in the press release and had asked the public to respect Roman's privacy during this difficult time. This had only added fuel to the fire and speculations were rife as to the exact relationship between Roman and the mystery man who'd saved him.

To James's relief, the scandal started to die down at the end of the first week.

Which made the black and silver Harley he found in his garage late Friday afternoon all the more pleasantly welcome. He'd left the door open when he'd driven out that morning.

James's heart skipped a beat as he parked his Jaguar next to Tristan's motorbike. He got out, closed the garage, and wiped his suddenly sweaty palms on his pants while he went around the bungalow.

Tristan rose from the steps of his porch, his helmet in hand.

"I asked Roman for your address and the code to your security gate," he confessed sheepishly.

James's mouth watered as he scanned the dark T-shirt stretched across Tristan's broad chest and the gray jeans hugging his strong legs.

"Sorry, I should have written those down for you the last time we met," he mumbled, his pulse quickening. "What kind of excuse did you give Roman?"

Tristan smiled, visibly relaxing. "Something about fixing your engine."

James's lips lifted in an amused grin. "I thought you weren't allowed to do that anymore."

Tristan arched an eyebrow. "I didn't say what engine I was intending to fix." He raked James with his gaze.

James's cock twitched to attention at the deliberate innuendo. He walked up the steps until he stood toe to toe with Tristan and arched an eyebrow.

"So, you're saying you want to look under my hood?"

Tristan's lips quirked. "I think you need the full service."

James laughed, his entire body lightening as the tension he'd lived with all week drained out of him.

Tristan always had that effect on him.

"I'm glad you came," he confessed in a heartfelt tone.

Tristan brushed their noses together and pressed a soft kiss to his mouth, his eyes twinkling warmly. "I thought it would make a nice surprise. You've had a shitty week by the sounds of things."

James laid his head against Tristan's shoulder, grateful for his strength. "It's not been the best."

Tristan looped his arms around James's waist and pulled him closer. "What can I do to make you feel better?" he murmured in his ear.

James shivered and angled his head to the side. Tristan accepted the silent invitation and kissed the side of his neck. Fire ignited in James's veins, raising goosebumps on his flesh.

"God, I love it when you do that," he sighed.

Tristan nibbled on his skin. "Is that the only thing you like about me?"

James's belly clenched at the silent question Tristan didn't voice.

He cupped the back of Tristan's head and pressed closer to him.

"No. I like everything about you."

James felt Tristan's surprise in the way he stiffened slightly against him. He waited breathlessly for his reaction, his heart pounding.

He'd never put himself on the line like this before. It should have scared the hell out of him. Yet, it didn't. And he knew that had everything to do with the man holding him in his arms.

"I'm glad," Tristan murmured in a fervent tone. "I like everything about you too."

James closed his eyes, more content than he could ever recall being in his entire life. Tristan shifted against him.

"James?"

"Yeah?"

"I really want you naked right now."

CHAPTER SIXTEEN

James shivered as Tristan's erection nudged his hip. Desire thickened his own cock. "Fuck!" He grabbed Tristan's butt and ground their groins together.

Tristan growled and bit down on his skin. "Yup, that's exactly what I'm intending to do to you tonight."

A wild look glazed James's face when Tristan raised his head. He fumbled for his house keys, grabbed Tristan's hand, and dragged him inside.

Tristan only had time to glance around the clean, modern interior before James shut the door and pushed his back against it. He chuckled.

"This feels familiar."

Color stained James's cheekbones. He clasped Tristan's head and gave him a kiss that made his toes curl.

Tristan took his glasses off and chased after his lips when he let go, his body feverish with need. James put his specs on a table in the hall and came back. He lowered his hands to Tristan's belt and unbuckled his jeans, his movements frantic.

Tristan groaned as James drew his zipper down and freed his erection. His pulse stuttered when James lowered himself to his knees.

"I've dreamt about sucking you for days," he confessed huskily.

A lusty curse left Tristan as James started exploring the silken skin and thick veins covering his engorged flesh with his fingers. He almost swallowed his tongue when James licked his tip and sucked down the side of his shaft to the root.

Tristan pressed his hands against the door and closed his eyes. He canted his hips forward, a shiver rippling through him as James repeated the sensual movement.

"Jesus, that feels amazing!"

James's throaty chuckle reached his ears.

Tristan opened his eyes in time to see his lips part and swallow the head of his dick. Pleasure slammed into him as he experienced the velvety depths of James's mouth for the first time. James wrapped his tongue around his shaft and sucked beautifully as he came off.

Tristan swore and fisted a hand in James's hair. He heard the sound of a buckle being undone and spied James freeing his erection.

James took Tristan back inside his mouth and groaned as he started rubbing himself briskly. He repeated the motion over and over, head bobbing to and fro until his jaw relaxed enough for him to be able to swallow Tristan to the back of his throat.

Sweat beaded Tristan's face as James took his time learning exactly how he liked to be blown. His chest shuddered with his ragged breathing, the intoxicating sounds their flesh made so damn arousing he committed them to memory.

Tristan finally caved in to his body's demands and gently thrust his hips, careful not to choke James. James grunted around his flesh and sucked harder. Tristan gritted his teeth as the most exquisite sensations flooded his sensitive nerve endings.

It was rare someone could deep-throat him like James was doing.

James looked up at him from under his lashes, his eyes a stormy green. His cheeks bulged and contracted as he worked Tristan's length.

The carnal picture he made where he knelt blowing him while he gave himself a brisk handjob had pleasure tightening Tristan's spine and balls. He hissed and cursed, the hot knot in his belly swelling as he neared his peak.

James moaned and stiffened before jerking and coming fitfully at Tristan's feet, his cum spurting onto the floorboards. The motions his tongue and jaw made as he climaxed tipped Tristan over the edge of his own orgasm.

He came on a harsh shout, his dick throbbing painfully as he clasped the back of James's head and spilled his cum inside his throat.

James gulped his seed greedily.

The way he licked his lips when he let go of Tristan's sensitive organ had Tristan groaning all over again. He pulled James to his feet and took his mouth in a scorching kiss. A mumbled curse left him when he tasted himself on James's tongue.

He let go of James and indicated a passage branching off the hallway to the left. "Is that the way to your garage?"

James's pupils contracted and dilated, his face flushed with excitement. "Yeah."

Tristan took James's hand and headed that way.

He flicked the overhead lights on when he entered the shadowy space, guided James to the Jag, and backed him up against the front grille.

"Is this where you gave yourself a handjob?" Tristan growled.

He leaned down, sucked on the pulse beating frantically at the base of James's throat, and pulled his left leg up over his thigh as he ground their naked cocks together.

"Yes!" James gasped. He arched deliciously and started riding Tristan's thigh in a delicious bump and grind that had them both cursing.

They kissed and touched one another with a roughness borne out of pure need, fingers kneading hard flesh and sensitive skin.

Tristan's hands trembled when he pulled back and stripped James of his clothes and shoes. James leaned his hands against the warm hood of his car and watched him sultrily while he kicked off his boots and shrugged out of his own clothes, his cock a glorious pink and his tip leaking fresh precum.

Tristan's pulse raced with a desire that threatened to overwhelm him as he took him in his arms once more. All he wanted to do was plunge his cock inside James's body like he'd dreamt about all week long and not come out until he'd made him scream in pleasure a few times. The way James clung to him and moaned as they kissed passionately told Tristan he wanted the exact same thing.

Tristan wrenched their mouths apart and spun James around, determined to fulfill one of his own fantasies.

A gasp left James when he found himself bent over the hood of his car.

Tristan rained hot kisses on his back. A shiver rippled down James's spine as he looked over his shoulder, his hooded gaze sultry with lust. His mouth parted on a low moan when Tristan slipped his thumbs in his cleft and spread him open.

Tristan dropped to his knees and cursed. James's exposed pucker was even prettier than the last time he'd seen it. He leaned in and teased the tight folds with the tip of his tongue.

CHAPTER SEVENTEEN

JAMES CRIED OUT AND CLUTCHED THE HOOD OF HIS CAR wildly. "Fuck!"

Tristan's dick throbbed as he worked James's entrance with his lips and tongue. James's hole gradually softened. Tristan pushed his furrowed tongue inside and ran it around the taut rim.

"*Oh God!*" James dropped a hand to his cock and gripped his shaft tightly.

The way he convulsed and grunted told Tristan he was experiencing a dry orgasm. Tristan pulled out and reached under James's body to caress his tight balls.

James whimpered and shuddered, his entire body blushing with pleasure.

Tristan kissed and bit his left ass cheek. "Has anyone ever rimmed you before?"

James looked at him over his shoulder and shook his head dazedly. "No!"

The untamed expression on his face had Tristan grabbing his own cock and giving it a painful tug.

"Do you like it?" he growled.

James hesitated a second before swallowing and nodding shakily.

Tristan groaned, parted James's hole with his thumbs, and went to town on his ass. The sounds James made as Tristan worked his opening almost made his self-control snap. He clenched his jaw and reached under James to stroke his cock as he stabbed his tongue in and out of him and circled his rim.

It wasn't long before James exploded, his keens fading to raspy gasps as he ejaculated beautifully over his car.

Tristan released his quivering cock and gave his twitching folds a final kiss before rising to his feet. He grabbed a condom and a packet of lube from his wallet.

James looked around at the sound of the foil tearing, his body trembling and sweat beading his flushed face. He met Tristan's heated stare, licked his lips, and shook his head.

Tristan stopped, his heart pounding violently at what he read in James's eyes. "Are you saying—?"

"Yeah." James lowered his gaze to Tristan's erection. "I want you bareback."

Tristan swallowed. He'd never taken a man raw before.

"I'm clean, if that's what you're worried about," James mumbled.

Tristan dropped the condom on the floor and opened the lube. "So am I."

James's chest heaved with excitement as he watched

Tristan lube up, his pupils so large they almost filled his eyes.

Tristan let go of his sensitive flesh, parted James's cleft, and speared his hole with two slick fingers. James dropped his head and moaned, fingers flexing on the hood of the car as he swallowed him to the knuckles. He hummed and canted his hips deliciously to and fro while Tristan readied him for penetration.

Tristan's skin prickled with a tight heat as he removed his fingers and crowded James's back. He spread him open, pressed the head of his bare cock to his hole, and breached his opening with a firm push.

They both groaned as he sank inside an inch.

"*Fuck!* You feel good!" James whimpered. "Your dick is so thick and hot!"

Tristan gnashed his teeth when he pressed against the inner band guarding James's passage. James shuddered. His insides gradually relaxed.

Tristan shivered as he pushed through and bottomed out.

He stilled, determined to fully savor this insane sensation. It was more than he could have imagined. Being inside James like this didn't just feel right.

It was perfect. Like they belonged.

James squeezed him gently.

Tristan cursed and gritted his teeth. Then he grasped James's hips and gave them both what they so desperately wanted.

Sweat dripped off his nose and chin as he punched his cock in and out of James's body. James undulated sensuously beneath him, heedless of the hot drops splashing onto his skin, his back and ass flexing beautifully as he met Tristan's thrusts.

Heat slowly knotted Tristan's belly. It expanded, tightening his thighs. His spine. His balls. The first wave of his orgasm washed deliciously over him.

He groaned, barely able to think beyond the lust and pleasure storming his senses.

James's moans rose to a crescendo as he neared his peak. He threw his head back and shouted out in ecstasy as he came all over his car, body growing rigid and ass clenching fitfully. Tristan hissed as the sweet convulsions pulsing through his insides kneaded his sensitive cock and pushed him over the edge.

He came on a feral grunt, back bowing and body rising until he stood on his toes. Tristan's vision flickered on a white haze of pure rapture as his cock swelled and exploded deep inside James. James whimpered and moaned as he drilled his ass with his convulsions, the way he squeezed Tristan's ejaculating shaft telling him he was relishing the sensation.

Tristan groaned and cursed as he continued thrusting through his long and deep orgasm, stunned by its savagery. It wasn't until he'd filled James with the last drop of his seed that he finally shuddered to a stop.

His ears buzzed in the warm silence that befell them, the only sounds shattering the hush their harsh pants. Tristan blinked as his awareness returned. He swallowed and leaned down to press a kiss between James's quivering shoulder blades.

"That was unreal," he breathed against his damp skin.

James swallowed and nodded, too spent to speak.

He gasped when Tristan carefully pulled out of him.

"Oh!" James stiffened. Hot cum oozed down his inner thigh.

Tristan groaned at the erotic sight. He fingered James's twitching hole.

James hummed and squeezed around him.

Tristan's spent cock throbbed on a wave of fresh arousal.

Jesus, I can't believe I'm getting hard again!

"We should clean you up," he murmured, reluctantly removing his finger.

James shivered. He turned, propped himself on the hood of his car, and spread his thighs open.

"How about another round?" He gazed at Tristan with fire in his eyes and stroked his swelling cock.

Tristan cursed as the delicious picture James made where he lay before him like an offering.

"You're asking for trouble." His eyes dropped to James's erection and his loose opening. His lips parted hungrily.

He could see the evidence of his pleasure still coating James's insides.

James reached down and tugged on Tristan's hardening shaft.

Tristan hissed, eyes almost rolling into the back of his head.

James leaned up and kissed him. "What I'm asking is for you to stick this inside me until neither of us can walk, Mr. Hart."

Tristan didn't have to be asked a third time.

CHAPTER EIGHTEEN

James woke up to the faint cry of seagulls coming through an open window and the sun warming his back. He blinked fuzzily and raised his head to squint at the clock on his nightstand.

It was past eleven a.m.

He tensed when he saw the empty sheets beside him.

Faint music drifted over from somewhere inside his house.

James's gaze found the overnight bag on the chair by the door. A goofy smile stretched his lips. He hugged his pillow.

Tristan was still here.

His mouth watered when the delicious aroma of freshly roasted coffee and toasted bagel wafted into the bedroom. James pushed up on his hands and knees to go find Tristan and froze. He slumped down on the sheets with a heartfelt groan.

His back hurt like crazy and his ass was on fire.

A grimace twisted his mouth as he carefully climbed out of bed.

He had no one to blame but himself for his current state. He was the one who'd seduced Tristan into fucking him five times last night. Heat warmed his face when he recalled their last, frenzied session in the shower. Tristan's gravelly voice had sounded pretty awesome as his colorful curses and grunts had echoed against the tiles.

James couldn't help grinning at the memory as he brushed his teeth. He put on sweatpants and a T-shirt and went in search of Tristan.

He found him at the kitchen island buttering a plateful of bagels.

Tristan had opted for black jeans and a white T-shirt that showcased his tanned skin and powerful muscles. James swallowed.

The man looked good enough to eat.

Tristan looked up and smiled when James padded barefoot around the island. "Hey." He pressed a soft kiss to James's mouth. "I was just coming to wake you up."

James melted against him and claimed his lips. They were both breathing a little fast by the time Tristan reluctantly lifted his mouth off his.

"Behave," he chided. He pushed a cup of coffee in James's hands.

James pouted and started climbing on a bar stool. He winced and stopped.

"And that is exactly why we should keep our hands off each other today," Tristan declared in a firm voice.

James grumbled as he followed Tristan out onto the terrace looking out over the swimming pool and garden. Tristan laid their breakfast on the outdoor table and pulled out a chair. He bit his lip as he watched the prudent way James lowered himself into it.

"Want an extra cushion?"

James narrowed his eyes. "Ha-ha."

Tristan chuckled and took the seat beside James. He gazed at the manicured lawn and colorful shrubs.

"This place is nice. I'd pegged you as living in a swanky apartment downtown."

James sucked in air with a fake shocked look. "Why, how prejudiced of you, Mr. Hart."

Tristan grinned and put a bagel in his mouth.

James crunched down on the toasted bread and sucked Tristan's thumb.

Tristan's eyes darkened. "The answer is no, James," he said gruffly, the flush of color staining his cheekbones a telltale sign he wasn't at all immune to James's seduction.

James leaned back and chewed his bagel with a grin.

"I didn't say a thing," he teased. He licked his lips.

Tristan's gaze arrowed hungrily on his mouth.

"I swear, you're gonna be sitting on a donut ring the rest of the week if I touch you today," he groaned.

James's eyes rounded. He burst out laughing at that mental picture.

A warm feeling spread through his chest as they sat in the sun and enjoyed their breakfast. He knew he was in way over his head and falling hard and fast for

Tristan. Yet, he wasn't scared in the least. Being with Tristan was as natural as breathing.

He sensed Tristan felt the same way.

The words that left his mouth next stunned him as much as they seemed to surprise Tristan. "You know, this is the first time I've had a guy stay over at my place."

Tristan finished swallowing the mouthful of coffee he'd just taken and carefully put his cup down. He studied him expectantly.

A bout of nervousness twisted James's stomach. Tristan reached over and took his hand. The quiet strength in his touch gave James the courage to confess his darkest secret to him.

"I was told I was frigid, a long time ago."

Tristan's fingers clenched around his.

"And which bastard told you that, exactly?" he said between gritted teeth.

"The man I slept with to land Crazyknot their first national tour."

The confession hung heavily in the space between them.

A muscle ticked in Tristan's cheek. "What?!"

James's throat tightened. He wondered if he'd made a terrible mistake.

"Shit!" Tristan leaned across and embraced him. "I'm not upset with you, James. I'm just angry at the asshole who pressured you into doing something that despicable!"

Relief shuddered through James. He squeezed his arms around Tristan's shoulders and burrowed his face in the crook of his neck. He'd always blamed himself for what had happened that awful night. And he'd thought others would blame him too.

It was clear Tristan felt the exact opposite.

"Who was it?" he said in a tight voice.

James swallowed. He pulled back and gazed into Tristan's haunted face. "I can't tell you that. Let's just say it was someone who could make or break Crazyknot's career."

"How old were you at the time?"

"Twenty-two," James admitted reluctantly.

"Fuck!" Tristan gnashed his teeth like he wanted to punch something.

"It happens a lot in this industry."

That statement didn't seem to make Tristan feel any better.

"Was it just the once?"

A self-deprecating smile stretched James's lips. "Yeah. He told me I was terrible in bed and never wanted to repeat the experience."

Tristan swore. "Is that why you said it had been a while? When we had sex the first time?"

James rubbed the back of his neck awkwardly. "I tried sleeping with other guys after that incident, but I could never enjoy the sex."

"Wait. Don't tell me—?!" Tristan paled and clenched his fists. "Did that asshole take your virginity?!"

James's eyes widened. He snorted, much to Tristan's chagrin.

"Sorry," he chuckled against Tristan's thin mouth. "Now you're really making me sound like a damsel in distress. I'm afraid Tyler Hillsby popped my cherry in the janitor's closet when I was seventeen."

Tristan frowned. "The janitor's closet?"

James shrugged. "There aren't many places to have sex at an orphanage." He kissed Tristan's tense jawline. "How old were you when you lost yours?"

Tristan gradually relaxed. "Fifteen."

James stared.

It was Tristan's turn to shrug. "I was an early bloomer."

"Let me guess," James joked. "It involved a garage."

Tristan blinked. "How did you know?"

James gaped. "Wait. You really lost your virginity in a garage?!"

"Dustin Franklin's dad bought a new Dodge," Tristan said like that explained everything.

James burst out laughing. Tristan smiled.

Just like that, the tension between them melted away.

"What do you want to do?" James asked as they cleared the table an hour later. "We can stay here and chill, or we can check out my hot tub." He indicated the tub under the arbor next to the swimming pool.

"And have you jump me while we're in it?" Tristan said drily. "I don't think so. How about I take you for a ride instead?"

James flashed him a seductive smile and trailed a lazy finger down his chest to his belt buckle. "You can ride me all you want, Mr. Hart."

Tristan groaned.

They went for a long ride along the coastline and

had lunch at a quaint seafood place James had never heard of before, but immediately became smitten with. He clung to Tristan's powerful body on the way back, the wind whipping at their clothes and the smile stretching his lips invisible behind his helmet. The way Tristan occasionally squeezed his hand where he clutched his midriff told him he was just as happy in that moment as he was. James closed his eyes, his heart swelling with emotion as he finally admitted the truth to himself.

This was love.

CHAPTER NINETEEN

Tristan looked up from his paperwork.

Leo McCormick stood in the doorway of his office. He was the youngest and most promising mechanic Tristan had hired in the past few years.

Surprise darted through Tristan when he glanced at the clock. "Sorry, I didn't realize it had gotten so late. You're the last one here?"

"Yeah. I've locked up." Leo made to leave, paused, and twisted on his heels. "So, you got plans this weekend?"

Tristan stared. It was rare for his employees to ask him about his private life.

"I'm not sure yet. Why?"

Leo wrinkled his nose. "Well, the guys and I were wondering if you were, you know…seeing someone."

Tristan arched an eyebrow.

"It's just—you kinda look happy lately," Leo added hastily.

Tristan digested this. "You mean, as opposed to being a depressing bastard?" he asked drily.

Leo flushed. "That's not what I meant. You—" he waved a hand vaguely, "well, you come across as this quiet, tough guy most of the time. But you seem more chilled these days. And you have a smile on your face all the time, like you're thinking about someone."

James's face flashed before Tristan. "Maybe I am."

Leo's eyes sparkled. "Oh! So you *are* dating someone?"

"Go home, Leo," Tristan grunted. "And tell the guys you lost the betting pool."

Leo's face fell. "How did you know there was a betting pool?"

Tristan blew out a sigh. "Because I know you assholes. I'm pretty sure this was Chase's idea."

"Wow," Leo mumbled. "You're a psychic *and* a mechanic."

Tristan pointed a commanding finger at the exit. "Home, Leo."

Leo trudged off, his shoulders slumped.

Tristan leaned back in his chair and rolled a pen between his fingers.

It was over a week since he'd last seen James. They'd spent that first Sunday lazing around reading the papers in bed and ended up in James's hot tub for a heavy session of handjobs and blowjobs before he'd reluctantly returned to Twilight Falls.

They hadn't been able to meet up the following weekend. James had committed Crazyknot to a couple of TV appearances while Tristan had had to drive to Santa Barbara to get some parts for his clients' cars.

I miss him.

His phone buzzed on his desk.

Tristan picked it up and couldn't stop the smile that stretched his mouth when he saw the name of the screen. "Hey."

"Hi," James said.

Tristan could tell he was smiling. "You just got home?"

"Yeah." Clothes rustled. "I'm free tomorrow night. Want to come over?"

Tristan imagined he was taking his tie and jacket off. "Sure. I was just thinking about you, actually."

"You were?"

Tristan grinned. He bet James's ears were turning pink just about now. "Yeah. I was wondering when I'd get to kiss you again."

A soft sigh traveled down the line. "Seems you're a mind reader. Was kissing me the only thing you thought about?" Springs squeaked softly.

"Are you in your bedroom?"

"Ah-huh. I'm just changing."

Tristan's dick stirred. "How about you stay naked?"

There was a soft indrawing of air. "What?" James mumbled.

Tristan's pulse quickened at the dirty fantasy taking shape in his mind. He pushed his chair back, crossed the office, and locked the door.

"I'm telling you to strip and sit on your bed, James."

James's breathing accelerated. The soft thunk of

shoes hitting floorboards reached Tristan's ears. Clothes swished.

He settled on his couch and massaged his erection as he pictured James getting naked for him.

"Sit down where you can see your mirror," Tristan ordered gruffly.

"Okay."

The springs creaked again.

Tristan pulled his zipper down. "Do you know what I'm doing right now, James?"

"No." Excitement raised the pitch of James's voice.

Tristan worked his erection out of his boxers and gave himself a slow tug. "I'm sitting on the couch in my office with my cock in my hand."

A sensual sound left James. Desire burned through Tristan.

"How about you spread your legs and pleasure yourself while I rub my dick?" he growled.

James's lewd moan sent a shiver down his spine.

"Are you touching yourself, James?"

"Y—yeah!"

Tristan bit his lip and thrust his shaft through his fingers. "Tell me how your cock looks."

James's shallow pants sounded in Tristan's ears. "It's hard. And pink."

Tristan's balls clenched at James's low groan. Blood pounded in his ears as he rubbed himself briskly. "What did you just do?"

"I—*Hmm!* I circled my slit with my thumb!"

Tristan's breathing grew labored as James's sinful description played across his vision. "Are you wet?"

A strangled sound left James. "Yes."

"Good. I'm getting wet for you too." Tristan smeared his palm with his precum and undulated his hips off his couch as he worked his erection. "I'm leaking so much for you, James."

James's filthy moans resonated in his ears. "Fuck! This feels so good!"

Pleasure tightened Tristan's body. He paused and squeezed the root of his cock. "Grab the lube, James."

Sheets swished. The soft slide of a drawer and a 'pop' came next.

"Tristan?"

Tristan clenched his jaw at the raw need in James's voice. "Why don't you slick two fingers and put them in your ass while we do this?"

James made a sound that raised goosebumps on Tristan's skin. His soft gasp a moment later told Tristan he was doing as he was told.

"Tell me what you see, James," Tristan groaned.

"I—My dick is so hard and red! I'm dripping precum on the sheets and I feel like I'm about to burst! And my fingers—*Oh!* My fingers feel so good inside my hole! I—I can't stop squeezing them!"

Tristan almost came then. He gripped his cock and counted to five as he fought for control.

"How about you rub that pretty cock of yours and fuck yourself nice and slow on your fingers?"

James whimpered.

Pleasure knotted Tristan's belly as he listened to the erotic sounds James made. He started stroking himself again.

James's breathing grew erratic. "Ah! Yes! Coming! Oh God! *I'm coming!*"

His shout of ecstasy had Tristan's spine tightening and his balls rising. He crested his own wave and stiffened and grunted as he ejaculated explosively all over his hand. A ringing filled his ears while he twitched and jerked, the waves of pleasure washing over him so fierce he barely heard his own grunts and James's wicked moans.

It was a while before Tristan could speak again. "James?"

"Yeah?" James panted.

"How about we go on a date tomorrow? You pick the place."

James groaned. "I can't believe you're asking me that when I've just had my fingers in my ass and my brain is still trying to process what we just did."

Tristan chuckled. He reached over for a tissue and wiped his hand. "So how about it?"

"Hmm. How about we go dancing?"

Tristan grinned. "You, hot and sweaty and writhing all over me? What's there not to like?"

CHAPTER TWENTY

Tristan's face fell a little when the cab pulled up outside the club.

"You okay?" James asked quizzically as he handed money to their driver.

"Yeah. I know the guy who owns this place."

James frowned at his expression. "You wanna go somewhere else?"

"It's alright." Tristan opened the door.

James raised an eyebrow as he stepped out of the vehicle after him. "I wouldn't have put Dan Flynn down as someone in your circle of friends."

"He isn't. He's a client."

They paid the entrance fee and headed inside.

Music rolled over James in a thumping wave when he and Tristan entered the main area.

The place he'd chosen for their first official date was reputed to be the hottest gay club in L.A.

They made their way to the bar and spotted Dan

Flynn talking to one of his staff at the far end. Dan's eyes widened at the sight of Tristan.

"Tristan!" He climbed off his stool and came over, a delighted smile stretching his mouth.

Tristan stiffened.

James stared curiously between the two men. His belly clenched when Dan touched Tristan's arm with a familiarity that suggested they were close. The club owner rose to press a warm peck on Tristan's cheek.

"It's great to see you." He squeezed Tristan's arm.

"Hi, Dan," Tristan muttered.

Dan pouted a little at his cool look. He finally registered James's presence and did a double take. "Oh, hey James."

"Dan," James greeted between clenched teeth, the jealousy prickling his skin as unexpected as it was vehement.

They knew each other through their shared connections to the music industry.

Surprise jolted James when Tristan slipped a possessive hand on the small of his back.

Dan noted the move with blatant interest. "Oh." He pursed his lips, his gaze swinging between them. "You two are—?"

"Yes, we are," Tristan replied steadily.

James's chest lightened at the proprietorial way Tristan said those words.

"Well, what do you know?" Dan mused. "I would never have pegged the two of you together." He blew out a sigh, defeat clearly pasted across his face. "Enjoy your night out, boys." He waved at them over his shoulder as he headed back to his chair.

James and Tristan got their drinks and found a free space by the wall.

"Before you ask, we've never had sex," Tristan said.

James took a sip of his beer and studied him inscrutably. "Not even a handjob?"

Tristan grimaced. "I told you, I don't mix business with pleasure."

He tensed when James leaned in and tugged his lower lip between his teeth.

"Good," James said huskily. "'Cause, I gotta say, I don't like seeing other men touch you."

Desire brightened Tristan's eyes. He looped an arm around James's waist and pulled him close.

"The feeling is mutual. Now, how about we finish these drinks and get on that stage?"

James complied hastily and soon find himself thrust inside the sea of bodies on a sunken floor. Tristan kept him close as they moved to the music, their chests and thighs touching tantalizingly while they skimmed each other's hips and ass with their hands. James's skin tingled and his cock ached at the delicious sexual tension sparking the air between them. The hooded look Tristan gave him told James he was just as turned on.

One of Crazyknot's most popular songs came on the speakers minutes later. The crowd went wild.

James gasped as he was jostled into Tristan's arms.

Tristan held him close. "I've got you."

James clung to him, his heartbeat loud in his ears.

The song was about unrequited lust. The men around them started bumping and grinding as they danced to the intoxicating beat.

Tristan tugged James through the heaving crowd and maneuvered him inside a shadowy alcove. He pressed James's back to the wall, grasped his thighs, and pulled him up against his body.

James gasped as he found himself riding Tristan's hips. He moaned when Tristan trapped his wrists above his head with a strong hand, nudged his chin up with his nose, and rained torrid kisses down the column of his throat.

"How many times did you touch yourself after what we did yesterday?"

James shivered as he recalled their scorching phone sex. He'd never done anything like that before. He hissed when Tristan bit down punishingly on his flesh.

"Tw—twice!" James gasped.

Tristan growled and started moving rhythmically to the music, his hips mimicking the act of sex as he thrust his erection against James's and suckled his neck. James tolerated the sweet torture for a breathless moment before grasping his face and yanking him up to take him mouth in a kiss full of animal need, his own body rolling to the seductive beat.

Tristan groaned and sank his fingers in James's ass where he held him, his tongue lashing seductively against James's eager flesh.

By the time the song ended, James was so close to coming, he knew all it would take was a single stroke of Tristan's fingers on his cock for him to explode.

They panted heavily as they rested against one another in the shadows. Tristan finally let go of James's wrists and slid him down his body. James shuddered and looped his arms around Tristan's neck when he felt the thick shape of his dick against his belly.

"That was crazy hot," he mumbled against Tristan's shoulder.

"Nope, that was Crazyknot," Tristan said in a deadpan tone.

James groaned. "Your puns are getting worse."

Tristan chuckled. "I'll take that as a compliment." He took James's hand and kissed his palm, his eyes gleaming with heat. "And yes, that was unreal. Everything we do together is unreal."

James swallowed at his candid expression. "I—" He froze in the next instant, his stomach clenching so violently he felt nauseous for a second.

No!

"James?" Concern clouded Tristan's face. He looked over his shoulder and followed James's horrified gaze.

Blood roared in James's ears as he stared at the man whose actions had destroyed his sex life for the better part of a decade. But it wasn't the sight of Maximillian Sutton that was turning his blood to ice. He'd seen the guy on many a social occasion before since they worked in the same town and industry. The mocking smirk Sutton occasionally flashed his way at the parties they'd attended had had James boiling with anger.

No, it was the fact that the music producer he was coerced into sleeping with seven years ago had his arm wrapped around the waist of a young, up and coming singer that had bile rising in James's throat.

TRISTAN PAID THE CAB DRIVER AND SLAMMED THE DOOR shut. He watched the vehicle disappear down the road before turning to look at the silent man beside him.

James's shoulders slouched as he opened the security gate to his home. He'd kept silent for most of the ride back, his expression stiff and his knuckles white on his lap while he gazed blindly out the window.

Tristan could guess the identity of the man James had stared at with an ashen face back at the club, before he'd told him he wasn't feeling well and wanted to go home.

James startled when Tristan silently clasped his hand as they walked up the drive to the bungalow. The way his fingers clenched around Tristan's made his chest ache.

A heavy hush settled between them when they entered the foyer.

Tristan guided James to the lounge, sat him on the

couch, and poured two glasses of whiskey from the drinks cabinet. He got some ice from the kitchen and returned to James's side.

James accepted the drink he handed him with a look of relief. "Thanks."

Tristan took the spot beside him and sipped his whiskey.

The alcohol burned a smooth path down his throat, much like the tension simmering in his veins. He was angry. Angrier than he could ever recall being in his entire life.

"That was him, wasn't it?" he finally said, keeping his tone neutral. "The music producer you slept with?"

James shuddered and nodded. He leaned his elbows on his knees and pressed his glass to his forehead.

"It's not like I haven't crossed paths with him before," he mumbled, his expression stark. "It was a given that I'd meet him again. But—that guy he was with tonight? He's new to the industry. In fact, he looks even younger than I was when that asshole approached me."

Rage warmed Tristan's body.

"You think he might do the same thing to him he did to you?" he asked between clenched teeth.

James swallowed. "I…don't know. I've asked around subtly over the years." He met Tristan's puzzled gaze. "To see if he had a habit of pressuring young men into sleeping with him to launch their music careers. Though there have been rumors of him sniffing around some of the new talent who've appeared on the music scene in the last decade, there's never been enough to pin anything on him." His expression turned haunted. "For all I know, that guy he was with tonight was with him consensually."

Tristan took their glasses, put them on a side table, and pulled James in his arms as he leaned back on the couch. James hugged him tightly.

The way he trembled had Tristan's stomach twisting.

"Do you really believe that?"

James hesitated before shaking his head.

"What do I do? Should—should I warn him?" he asked in a frail voice.

Tristan tipped his chin up with knuckle and gazed steadily in his eyes.

"What's your gut telling you to do?"

"It's telling me to knock that bastard's lights out," James blurted out.

Tristan blinked. He chuckled in the next instant. "Alright, besides that, Superman?"

James chewed his lip. "I should talk to that singer."

Tristan nuzzled his nose. "I agree. This will eat you up if you don't do something about it."

James nodded. He pressed his face against Tristan's shoulder.

"Do you know what I hate the most about what happened tonight?" he mumbled after a while.

"What?"

"I was so close to coming after we did that bump and grind," James confessed with heartfelt regret. "Like, all it would have taken is your hand on my cock and I would—" A strangled sound left him when Tristan stood up, pulled him to his feet, and bent to hook his arms under his knees.

James gasped when Tristan hefted him effortlessly in a fireman's lift and marched toward the bedroom. He laughed. "Why do I get the feeling I just touched a sore spot?"

"I'm gonna touch all your spots, inside and out," Tristan pledged fervently.

"Promises, promises," James teased.

Tristan placed him on his feet in the middle of the bedroom and took his jacket and T-shirt off. "How about you keep still and let me eat you?" He unzipped James's jeans, yanked them down his thighs, and knelt to take him inside his mouth.

James groaned lustfully as Tristan swallowed his cock to the back of his throat in one fell swoop. He sank his fingers in Tristan's hair and moaned when he started sucking him, his punching hips soon adding to the sublime friction.

It didn't take long for him to come.

Tristan let go of his spent cock, finished undressing both of them, and pushed him face down on the bed, his expression raw with need. James's heart thundered against his ribs as Tristan grabbed the lube from the nightstand and hurriedly prepped him.

They both cursed when Tristan framed his hips with his knees and finally sank his cock inside his hole.

Tristan secured James's arms above his head and fucked him hard and deep, his undulating hips crushing James deliciously into the bed while he rutted against him. The frame shuddered with his thrusts, the squeak of the springs and his passionate grunts so erotic James climaxed within a minute of Tristan being inside him.

He came one more time before Tristan finally found his release, his feral groans echoing hoarsely around the bedroom as he pinned James to the bed and spilled his seed inside him with frenzied jerks of his hips.

James's heart raced like a freight train when Tristan pulled out, flipped him on his back, and entered him again, still rock hard. He leaned down and kissed James, his face flushed and his expression wild with lust.

"Hang on to me!"

James locked his legs around Tristan's waist as Tristan pulled him up into his arms. He found himself straddling Tristan's lap and moaned when the new position lodged Tristan's cock even deeper inside him.

Sweat coursed down Tristan's face as he held James's hips and stroked his dick in and out of him. James clung on to his shoulders and accepted everything he gave him, their heavy pants filling the scant space between their bodies.

This was more than just sex.

This was Tristan marking him as his.

James wasn't sure if it was jealousy or possessiveness that had triggered Tristan's animal side tonight. To be truthful, he didn't care. He just relished the potent lovemaking, knowing it was something rare and utterly precious despite its sweet savagery.

It was a few hours before dawn when they collapsed on the bed, their dicks finally spent and James's passage aching pleasantly from the intense carnal mating his body had been subjected to. As he rested his head against Tristan's chest and let the strong beat of his heart lull him to sleep, he realized he'd forgotten all about Maximillian Sutton and the ugly emotions his past mistake always invoked in him.

CHAPTER TWENTY-TWO

"So, how are things going with you and Roman?" Tristan asked lightly.

Drake paused in the act of unwrapping a banner and shot a glance at Hunter and Nathan where they were blowing up balloons and putting up streamers in Elaine's dining room. He studied Tristan steadily.

"That's a bit out of left field."

"It isn't really," Tristan said with a shrug. "You brought him to see Miles, remember? I think that made your relationship pretty clear to everyone."

Drake pulled a face. He finished unwrapping the banner.

"It's—" He faltered, his expression growing sheepish. "To be honest, it's going so well, it's kinda scaring me."

Tristan bit back a smile. Drake being nervous about his relationship with Roman could mean only one thing. He was in love with the rock star.

Whether he was aware of that yet was another matter.

Drake had a nasty habit of shooting himself in the foot when it came to his relationships, the prime example being how he'd messed things up with Alex before the lawyer had left Twilight Falls to pursue a career in San Diego.

Roman's return to L.A. at the end of his staycation in Twilight Falls had been all over the entertainment channels a few weeks ago, as well as news of Crazyknot being back in the studio to record a brand-new album. It had finally put to rest the speculations about the mystery man who'd saved Roman from his criminal father.

Drake climbed on a chair and lifted the banner. "Here?"

Tristan bobbed his head. "Yeah, that looks good."

He helped Drake fix the strip to the arch separating Elaine's kitchen from her dining room. They stepped back and examined the gaily decorated rooms critically.

Miles was finally coming home today. The Terrible Seven et al. had been getting ready for his surprise welcome party all week. The showpiece was the cake Elijah had made, along with the delicious food he'd prepared with Sam and Izzy's help the night before.

"He's gonna faint when he sees this," Nathan said.

Hunter finished blowing up a balloon and grinned. "Yeah, well, we didn't get to celebrate his birthday all those years, so he's having everything in one go." He indicated the enormous pile of gifts sitting at the end of Elaine's dining room with a proud grin.

They'd bought Miles everything they would have gotten him for each of his birthdays and every Christmas he'd missed.

Alex appeared. "His room's ready."

Finn wiped paint streaks from his hands as he followed him inside the room.

Elijah brightened when he came through the back door with a box of prepped food and saw Finn. "The mural's done?"

"Yup."

Alex kissed Finn. "My husband's a genius."

Elijah sighed, put the carton on the counter, and covered Maisie's eyes when she came into the kitchen with Carter. Maisie peeled his fingers off her face and watched eagerly as Alex and Finn locked lips.

"I'm gonna marry Uncle Miles when I grow up," she declared to her fathers. "And we'll do smoochies, just like that!" She pointed at Alex and Finn.

Carter nearly dropped what he was carrying. "What?" he protested. "I thought you were gonna marry us when you grow up." He indicated himself and Elijah with a wounded look.

"Don't be silly, daddy," Maisie chided, causing several of them to bite their lips. "You're too old for me."

"I hate to break it to you, kid, but your Uncle Miles is the same—" The rest of Hunter's words were muffled when Theo came up behind him and clamped a hand over his mouth.

The familiar sound of Elaine's Chevy rose from the driveway.

"Quick, hide!" Alex hissed.

They crowded behind the dining room door. Footsteps sounded on the porch a moment later.

"Maybe we should install a ramp," Elaine said as she opened the front door.

"I'll be fine, Mom," Miles said. "Besides, I need the exercise."

"You're doing great," Izzy reassured.

Tristan and the others waited until the three of them came into the kitchen before jumping out from behind the door.

"Surprise!"

Miles rocked back on his heels at their welcome shouts, eyes rounding and finger tightening on his walking stick. He stared at the gaily decorated rooms before looking accusingly at Elaine and Izzy. "You knew?!"

"Of course." Izzy grinned proudly. "It was my idea."

Miles groaned and flushed as everyone came over to hug him.

The rest of the day passed in a blur of laughter and happy moments Tristan knew they would all cherish forever more. Elaine lined Elijah's cake with candles and everyone snorted when Maisie helped Miles blow them out. Miles looked dazed when he opened all their gifts after they'd eaten, his face flushed and his eyes glistening with tears.

It was late afternoon by the time Tristan and the

others got ready to leave. Tristan looked at his watch as he headed for his pickup. He smiled.

Just in time.

James was coming over tonight.

He spotted Miles and Drake talking quietly by Drake's motorbike while he started the engine. A haunted look crossed Miles's face. Drake hugged him and left, his expression equally tight. Miles watched him long after he'd disappeared.

Tristan frowned as he drove home.

What was that about?

James was sitting on the porch swing drinking a beer when he parked outside his lodge. He was dressed in jeans and a teal T-shirt that complemented his eyes.

"Hey." Tristan crossed the porch and pulled him up for a kiss.

James melted against him with a heartfelt sigh.

"How was the party?" he murmured when Tristan reluctantly lifted his mouth off his.

Tristan smiled. "It was great." He tugged James down onto the swing.

They sat in comfortable silence and watched the sun light up the lake as it started to set.

"Did it go okay with that singer?" Tristan asked after a while.

James dropped his head on Tristan's shoulder. "I made the decision to approach him directly rather than go through his agent. I thought it would be better coming straight from me." He sighed. "He didn't want to believe me at first. But he agreed to meet with me again. He's part of the opening act at a charity gig Crazyknot is headlining in ten days."

They talked well after dusk had fallen, their fingers interlaced. And when Tristan led James up to his bedroom later that night and made love to him, the truth that had slowly settled in his heart in the past few weeks resonated deeply inside him once more.

James was the man he wanted to spend the rest of his life with.

CHAPTER TWENTY-THREE

A PERSISTENT BUZZING WOKE JAMES UP EARLY THE NEXT morning. He blinked his eyes open.

His cell phone was vibrating on Tristan's nightstand.

Tristan's steady breaths ruffled his nape where he slept with one arm wrapped loosely around his waist. James was careful not to rouse him as he reached over and checked the caller ID.

It was Roman.

He frowned. As far as he knew, Roman was meant to be seeing Drake this weekend.

Why is he calling at this time?

The phone stopped buzzing. It started ringing again.

James gently lifted Tristan's arm and slipped out of bed, a sliver of unease tightening his chest. He padded barefoot out of the room and headed up the corridor to the landing overlooking the first floor and the huge windows facing the lake. The sun painted orange and pink streaks across the sky and the still waters as it rose over the San Bernardino Mountains.

James barely registered the pretty landscape while he answered Roman's call. "Hey."

"I'm outside your house."

James startled. "What?"

Roman's voice trembled. "I broke up with Drake last night."

James's stomach flip-flopped.

Warm arms wrapped around his waist from behind. Tristan pressed up against his back and kissed his shoulder.

"James? You there?" Roman said in his ear.

James's knuckles whitened on his cell. "Yeah, I am. I'll be there as soon as I can." He disconnected, turned in Tristan's hold, and met his wary gaze. "I'm sorry, I have to go." A muscle jumped in his cheek. "Drake and Roman broke up."

Surprise widened Tristan's eyes. "What? But I thought things were going pretty well between them."

James blew out a frustrated sigh. "So did I. I have no idea what happened exactly, but Roman is at my place right now." He leaned his head against Tristan's shoulder, remorse twisting his insides. He hated that he was putting Roman ahead of Tristan and his own needs. "I'll make it up to you, I promise."

Tristan stroked his back gently before tipping his chin up with a knuckle.

James expected to see reproach and maybe even resentment in his eyes. Instead, Tristan studied him with a patience and acceptance that made his heart swell with emotion.

"There's only one thing I would like for you to promise me," Tristan said quietly.

"What?" James's pulse raced at the way Tristan was looking at him.

Tristan leaned in and kissed him softly.

Desire stirred languorously through James.

Tristan ended the kiss and hugged him close. "That you'll consider making me your number one."

James's breath locked in his throat.

"You don't have to give me an answer right away," Tristan said in his hair. "I know Roman is your best friend and he needs you right now. If it was Hunter or any of the others who'd called, I'd be doing the same thing."

James pulled back a little, his heart thumping so hard his body almost vibrated. He framed Tristan's face in his hands and stared into his beautiful eyes.

"You don't have to wait for my answer," he quavered. "I love you. I've been in love with you for—"

The rest of his words were swallowed by Tristan's lips. This kiss wasn't soft, nor was it gentle. It was a passionate declaration. A promise of a future James had never dared dream of.

Tristan's pupils were bright and his face flushed with emotion when he lifted his mouth off James. "I love you too. I want to spend the rest of my life with you, James Lang."

His expression softened at the sound James made.

He kissed the tears blossoming on James's eyelashes, clasped his hand, and pressed hot lips to his palm.

"I want to tell my friends about you. I want to show the world that you're mine."

James sniffed and nodded shakily. "Okay." Tristan's faint smile had him looking at him questioningly. "What?"

"Your crying face is starting to grow on me."

James groaned. Tristan laughed and kissed his brow.

He insisted on feeding him toast and coffee before he left for L.A. By the time James pulled up on his driveway, it was past eight a.m.

Roman was sitting on his porch, his back against the wall and his head resting atop his knees where he hugged them to his chest. He jumped at the sound of his name and lifted his face.

James's heart contracted at the rock star's puffy eyes and ashen complexion. "You should have gone inside."

"I forgot your key," Roman mumbled.

James let him inside the house and closed the door. He turned to find Roman squatting on the floor in his hallway, his shoulders quaking with his muffled sobs. He swallowed the lump in his throat, dropped down on his haunches, and silently took his best friend in his arms.

IT WAS IZZY WHO ACCIDENTALLY REVEALED WHAT HAD happened between Drake and Roman when Tristan bumped into her at Elijah's bakery two days later.

He hadn't heard from James the rest of that Sunday or the Monday bar a brief message to say Roman was staying at his place for a couple of days.

He decided to grab lunch in town and found Izzy sitting at their regular table at the back of Elijah's shop. She was muttering under her breath while scrolling through her cell phone, her brow furrowed.

"What's got your panties in a twist?" Tristan said lightly.

Izzy startled when he took the seat opposite her. "Oh. Hey." Her frown returned. "My panties aren't in a twist."

"Yeah, they are."

Izzy let out a long suffering sigh and rolled her eyes. "Alright, they are, smartass." She chewed her lip and studied Tristan shrewdly. "You wouldn't happen to know anyone in L.A. who might have Crazyknot's schedule for the coming month, do you?"

Tristan finished chewing the mouthful of savory pastry he'd just taken and took a leisurely sip of his soda while he debated whether to tell Izzy the truth. He recalled what he'd said to James on Sunday morning, on the subject of telling his friends about them.

"I might."

Izzy stared. "You do?!"

Tristan shrugged. "I can ask James."

Izzy blinked, her expression growing blank. "James?" she said slowly. "You mean, James Lang?"

"Yeah." Tristan waited for the penny to drop. It didn't take long.

Izzy pressed a hand to her mouth and gasped, her eyes round. "You and James are fucking!"

Her squeal lowered the noise level in the shop by several decibels. Tristan winced as everyone looked their way.

Sam popped her head out of the kitchen door and scowled at Izzy.

"Sorry," Izzy mouthed guiltily at the bakery manager.

Elijah's voice came through faintly as the door swung shut behind Sam. "Who did she say was sleeping with—?!"

Izzy waited until the people around them were no longer gawking before leaning across the table, her green eyes sparkling. "You and the Ice Princess?! How'd that happen?!"

"It just did," Tristan replied laconically. "And don't call him the Ice Princess."

"Wow." Izzy stared. "It's serious, isn't it?"

"Yes."

Izzy made a face. "Well, at least you won't mess things up like Drake."

Tristan hesitated. He had a suspicion he knew what Drake had done.

"Did he tell Roman he wasn't interested in a long term relationship by any chance?" he hazarded.

"Bingo." Izzy sighed. "There's no one like Drake for screwing up his own love life. Did you know he went to see Alex and Finn on Saturday night?" She wrinkled her nose. "Alex said he cried."

Tristan's belly clenched at her words. The last time

he'd seen Drake shed tears was the night Miles went into a coma.

"Why do you want to know Crazyknot's schedule?"

Izzy tapped a finger on the table. "Because Alex and I have convinced that idiot to see the error of his ways. We just need the right opportunity for Drake to apologize to Roman and make things right between them."

Tristan hesitated. "I know Crazyknot is headlining a charity gig next week. I can get the details from James."

Izzy beamed. "That'd be great." Her smile faded to a grimace. "Also, you should tell Hunter. If he finds out I knew about you and James first, he'll sulk for months."

Tristan sighed. Izzy was right.

He called Hunter that afternoon and told him he was going out with James. Hunter turned up at his garage exactly fourteen minutes and thirty-six seconds later and wouldn't leave until he got every last juicy detail out of Tristan.

"So, it's serious, huh?" Hunter stared at him as they sat over coffee in his office, his expression grave.

Tristan nodded. "Yeah."

Hunter poked him in the ribs with an elbow. "You guys getting shacked up?"

Tristan grunted and winced. "We haven't broached that subject yet. A lot's happened."

Hunter pulled a face and rubbed his chin. "Ah. Crazyknot. You might have a tough time competing with them."

Tristan smiled faintly as he recalled the look on

James's face when he'd confessed his love to him. "Somehow, I think I'll be okay."

Hunter grimaced. "Man, I've never seen you look so sappy. What happened to my strong and brooding best fr—*Ouch!*"

Tristan let go of his ear.

He didn't have to ask James about the charity gig in the end.

James called him that night and invited him to the afterparty.

CHAPTER TWENTY-FOUR

MUSIC POUNDED IN THE DISTANCE, ALONG WITH THE noise of the frenzied crowd. The mood at the charity concert was electric and the main act hadn't even gotten on stage yet.

James knew tonight's turnout wouldn't just benefit the organization at the heart of the two-hour long music production. It would be a boon for the artists involved in the opening act too.

He opened the door to Crazyknot's dressing room to find them chanting their familiar pre-stage war cry.

"That never gets old," James said with a wry smile. "Now, how about you get out there and show these people a good time?"

Roman's face tensed up a little as he led the way out of the dressing room. As the focus of their band, he always got nervous before a performance. But James knew he'd be okay once he got on stage. It was like he became someone else when he was under the glare of the spotlights.

Relief shot through him when he studied Roman out of the corner of his eyes. The darkness that had haunted the rock star's eyes had subsided.

Though he was still grieving the end of his relationship with Drake, he was no longer the hot mess he'd been those first few days he'd stayed over at James's place. The rest of the band had finally clocked on to what had happened and had come over to cheer him up.

Today was the first time Crazyknot would be live on stage since the scandal about Roman's father broke out. They'd finished recording their latest album in record time and intended to play two new songs at tonight's charity gig, ahead of the album's official release next month.

James watched from the wings as Crazyknot launched into their opening number. From the way the crowd reacted, he was confident it would make the top of the music charts and stay there for some time.

Tristan's face danced in front of his eyes. A warm feeling lightened his entire body as he relived the last time they'd been together. He still couldn't believe they'd confessed their feelings for one another or how incredibly natural it had been for them to do so.

He knew he had Tristan's sincerity and steadfastness to thank for that.

They had made it easy for James to open up to him and accept the possibility of their relationship. Though he knew he could count on his childhood friends to help him in his time of need, he'd always been the backbone of their group. The one everyone else came to when they had a problem. It had been like that at the orphanage too.

The fact that he could rely on someone like Tristan had made James realize he didn't have to act strong all the time. That he could have his moments of weakness and share them with someone he trusted wouldn't judge him.

Their love was a rare gift, one that they both equally cherished.

It had been hard to keep his new relationship a secret from Roman and the rest of Crazyknot this past week. All he'd wanted to do was shout it from the rooftops.

But he couldn't do that to Roman, not when he was still suffering from his recent breakup.

James's pulse quickened when the band neared the close of their second song. He checked his cell phone as he headed backstage. Tristan had texted an hour ago, before he'd left Twilight Falls. Which meant he would be in L.A. soon.

James smiled. He couldn't wait to see him.

Anxiety tightened his belly for a moment. He still had an unpleasant task to deal with at the afterparty. He hoped he would be able to talk some sense into the young singer Maximillian Sutton had approached.

James had just reached Crazyknot's dressing room when the last man he'd expected to see tonight came marching up the corridor.

"Drake?" His eyes rounded as he clocked Drake's

dark grey morning suit and the bouquet of roses in his hand. "Wait. Is this what I think it is?!"

Drake stopped in front of him and dipped his head. "I intend to apologize to Roman and propose to him."

The way he clenched his jaw and gripped the flowers told James he really meant what he'd said.

"You hurt him," James said accusingly. "Badly."

Regret darkened Drake's eyes. "I know. And I'll spend the rest of my life making it up to him, I swear."

The sound from the auditorium built to a crescendo. Crazyknot had just finished on stage.

James blew out a sigh. "Get in there before I change my mind."

He indicated the dressing room with a jerk of his head.

Emotion brought a flush of color to Drake's face. "Thanks."

Roman appeared at the head of the band minutes later. He slowed when he saw James standing outside the dressing room and gave him a puzzled look.

James looked past his shoulder to Kurt and the others. "Can we give Roman a moment? There's someone in there waiting to speak to him."

"Who's waiting for me?" Roman said, confused.

James shrugged, hoping his tone didn't betray him. "It's a kid the charity chose to meet with you."

Roman glanced at their equally bewildered friends. "Then, shouldn't we all meet him?"

"No. He wanted to see you alone."

Suspicion furrowed Roman's brow. "There had

better not be an inflatable sex doll in there, like that time we toured in France," he said, irate.

Lewis snorted.

"Just—get in there!" James grabbed Roman, opened the dressing room, and shoved him inside before slamming the door shut in his face.

The rest of the band stared at him like he'd lost his mind.

"What's really going on, James?" Kurt frowned and crossed his arms.

James rubbed the back of his neck. "Drake's here."

Lewis sucked in air.

"What?" Hugo said in a strained voice.

"Wait. He's not here to propose, right?" Robbie joked.

James stared. "How'd you know?"

Everyone including Robbie gaped at him.

"Drake's proposing?!" Lewis squealed.

They scowled and hushed him as several of the backstage crew looked their way quizzically.

Lewis pressed his ear against the door, undeterred.

"What are you doing?!" Kurt hissed.

Lewis rolled his eyes. "What does it look like I'm doing, Sherlock? I'm eavesdropping."

James groaned when the others glanced at one another and unashamedly following suit. "You guys!"

"Get over here!" Kurt yanked on his arm.

James stumbled into him.

The door opened abruptly under their combined weight.

They tumbled inside the dressing room and crashed unceremoniously onto the floor. Lewis groaned at the bottom of the pile of bodies.

"I told you assholes not to do that," James grumbled where he lay on top.

They scrambled to their feet under Drake and Roman's narrow-eyed stares.

"So, did he say yes?" Kurt asked Drake eagerly.

"I didn't get a chance to finish proposing," Drake said darkly, still on one knee.

Roman scowled.

The rest of Crazyknot had the grace to look abashed.

"Well, don't let us stop you," James said as he dusted himself off.

Drake and Roman stared at them like they'd grown a second head.

"Look, we're the closest thing you've got to a family and we should be here for this," Kurt told Roman in a tone that would not be denied.

Roman's shoulders deflated. He met Drake's gaze. "They're right."

Drake sighed. "Okay." He cleared his throat again. "Dear Roman Campbell—and irritating family—"

"Hey!" Kurt protested.

Drake ignored the guitarist, his gaze full of emotion as he stared at Roman. "Will you grant me the honor of becoming my husband?"

Roman's chin quivered. "Yes."

James's heart contracted at the sheer happiness radiating in his best friend's eyes.

Everyone choked up when Drake took Roman's left hand and slipped a beautiful platinum band on his ring finger.

"Oh shucks, you guys!" Lewis wailed. "You're gonna make me bawl!"

Kurt passed him a tissue.

CHAPTER TWENTY-FIVE

Tristan showed his phone to one of the people manning the entrance of the hotel. The place wasn't far from the concert's venue and had views out over Venice Beach and Santa Monica Pier. The woman checked his electronic pass and let him through.

The private afterparty was being held in a ballroom at the back of the hotel. Tristan walked inside the bustling hall and scanned the sea of people. He spotted James talking to a group of men and women at the far side of the room and made his way over.

James's face brightened when he saw him through the crowd. He excused himself and closed the distance to Tristan at a brisk pace.

"Hey." He stopped in front of him, his green eyes sparkling.

Tristan smiled, the warm feeling oozing through his chest as familiar as his own breath. "Hey, yourself."

James's lips parted a little as he scanned Tristan's

dark suit and red silk shirt. "You scrub up real nice, Mr. Hart."

Tristan leaned in and brushed his lips against James's ear. "That's because I'm trying to impress you, Mr. Lang."

The way James shivered and angled his head slightly told Tristan he was well on his way to getting hard.

Kurt appeared. "Oh, hi Tristan." He gave him a quizzical look. "I didn't know you'd been invited to the afterparty."

Hugo, Lewis, and Robbie weren't far behind him.

James turned to face his friends. He took a deep breath and clasped Tristan's fingers. "He's my guest."

Kurt blinked. "Huh?"

"Oh." Understanding dawned in Robbie's eyes.

Tristan lifted James's hand and kissed his knuckles before slipping a proprietary arm around his waist. "Just in case that wasn't clear, he means we're a couple."

Lewis choked on his champagne.

"Wow," Hugo mumbled while Kurt grimaced and slapped the drummer's back. "First Roman and Drake, now you two."

Tristan tensed. "What happened between Roman and Drake?"

"Drake proposed," James told him with a soft smile. "Roman said yes."

"Oh." Tristan stared, a little stunned. "I knew he was coming to apologize to Roman. I didn't know he was going to propose."

"He even got our permission," Kurt said curtly. His

gaze still held a degree of wariness as he looked from James to Tristan. "No offense, but I'd never have pegged the two of you getting together. Not in a million years."

"None taken," Tristan drawled. "And you're not the first person to say that."

"Yeah," Lewis mumbled, his voice still raw with surprise. "I mean, you're Mr. Sex on Legs and he's Mr. Prim and Proper." He pointed at James.

James narrowed his eyes.

Tristan flashed them a wicked smile. "Want to know something?"

"What?" Kurt said warily.

Tristan beckoning them close with a crooked finger.

Crazyknot leaned in.

"Mr. Prim and Proper is absolute fire between the bedsheets," Tristan whispered.

Kurt and Hugo sucked in air. Lewis and Robbie gawped.

James groaned and blushed. "I can't believe you just said that." He punched Tristan lightly on his arm.

"It's the truth," Tristan chuckled. He kissed James's hair. "We need to shatter that Ice Princess impression people have of you, starting tonight. I want them to realize what a precious gift they've overlooked all those years and drool with jealousy now that you're mine."

James bit his lip, his expression turning sultry at Tristan's possessive tone.

"Sheesh, get a room," Kurt mumbled.

James startled when the guitarist hugged him.

"I'm happy for you," Kurt said tightly. "Still, I don't know why you felt you had to keep this a secret from us. You have to tell Roman."

James squeezed his arms around Kurt, remorse bringing a lump to his throat. "I will."

Movement caught his gaze.

Eddie Sandford, the singer Maximillian Sutton had approached, had come up behind Robbie. He hesitated as he met James's eyes.

James let go of Kurt. "Hi, Eddie," he said in a light tone. "Want to have that talk?"

Eddie nodded. Unease flitted through James.

The singer had a haunted look in his eyes.

Eddie froze when someone slipped an arm around his waist.

James bit back a curse. Tristan stilled beside him.

"There you are." Maximillian Sutton's gaze swept James and Crazyknot dismissively. He gave Eddie a saccharine smile. "How about we head outside for a bit?"

He guided the singer toward the doors leading out onto the terrace and the beach. Eddie cast a glance at James over his shoulder a second before he vanished into the night.

James scowled. "Fuck."

"James?" Kurt frowned while the others exchanged confused looks.

"We should go after them," Tristan said stiltedly. "That kid looked scared."

James nodded.

They headed in the direction the pair had

disappeared. Darkness swallowed them when they exited the terrace and stepped onto the beach. They stopped some hundred feet from the hotel and scanned the shadowy landscape.

"There." Tristan pointed at a beach hut to the left.

James clenched his jaw when he made out two indistinct figures locked in an embrace. They reached the shack in time to see Eddie shove Maximillian away.

"I said no, dammit!" The singer's voice trembled as he glared at the music producer. He wiped his mouth. "James was right. You're nothing but a vulture. I won't let you touch me again!"

James's blood turned to ice. *No!*

Maximillian's expression grew ugly. "James? You mean, James Lang?" he spat. "He's the only reason Crazyknot are as successful as they are today. And he has me to thank for that." A harsh bark left him. "Although the guy was frigid in bed, at least he offered his ass to me when I asked for it."

"You fucking asshole," Tristan growled. He stormed toward Maximillian.

The music producer startled when he registered their presence.

James got to him before Tristan and punched him in the jaw.

Maximillian grunted and staggered backward. His wild gaze found James. "What the—?!"

James ignored his throbbing fist and marched up to the man who had made his private life a living hell for the better of his adult existence. He grabbed him by the scruff of his thousand-dollar suit and looked him straight in the eye.

"The reason I lay like a statue in that bed is because you're a lousy lover and you couldn't turn me on," James hissed. "Just like you probably couldn't arouse any of the guys you forced to have sex with you." He pushed him violently.

Maximillian fell on his backside, his expression stunned. He recovered and glared at James and Eddie. "So what? It's your word against mine. And everyone in this town knows my word is law."

Tristan gnashed his teeth. "This arrogant fucker."

James pressed a hand against his chest as he took a step toward Maximillian. "Don't. He's not worth an iota of your attention."

"I'm afraid that's where you're wrong, *Maxie*." Eddie joined James, his eyes shooting daggers and his body quivering with adrenaline and rage. He took his cell phone out of his pocket. "I recorded tonight's little incident, as well as what happened between us yesterday, when you forced a kiss on me. It's no longer your word against ours, dipshit."

Horror widened Maximillian's eyes. He lunged for Eddie's phone.

Eddie scowled, batted his arm away, and kicked him in the crotch.

They glared collectively at the man as he howled and bent over, hands clutching his balls.

"You did good, kid," Tristan told Eddie with a grunt.

Eddie sagged, the fight draining out of him. James steadied him as he swayed.

"Was it just a kiss?" James peered at him anxiously. "He didn't do anything else?"

Eddie shuddered and shook his head. "No. I told him I was on my period and left."

Tristan snorted. Relief made James lightheaded.

"James?" someone shouted in alarm behind them. "Is everything okay?"

They turned.

Kurt and the rest of Crazyknot were rushing across the beach toward them, a couple of security guards on their heels.

James took a shaky breath and steadied his nerves. His stomach fluttered when Tristan laid a comforting hand on the small of his back.

"We need to call the cops and report an assault," James told the security guards in a hard voice.

Kurt stared at the groaning man on the ground. "Did someone hit him?"

"Yeah, they did." Tristan cocked a thumb at James and Eddie, a proud smile playing on his lips.

Crazyknot gaped.

Eddie sniffed. "Asshole totally deserved it."

CHAPTER TWENTY-SIX

"*You idiot!*" Roman yelled.

James winced. Tristan squeezed his shoulders where he sat beside him on the couch.

"Calm down, Roman," Kurt said stiffly.

Roman glared at the guitarist before scowling at James.

Remorse twisted James's stomach.

It was the day after the charity concert.

Following Maximillian Sutton's arrest, James had contacted Eddie's agent and lawyer and requested they meet him and the singer at Crazyknot's agency to talk with their PR and legal teams. He knew the scandal he and Eddie were about to get dragged into would last months and likely involve a lawsuit against Maximillian. James intended to make sure they went about this the right way from day one, not just for his and Crazyknot's sake, but for Eddie's too.

By the time James and Tristan made it to his place in the early hours of the morning, news of

Maximillian's arrest was already on social media. By dawn, it had made local headlines.

The outpouring of support James received via private messages and on social media throughout that day fairly stunned him and had him choking back tears. He hadn't realized how much the people in his industry admired and respected him. And not just that.

They believed him and Eddie.

So far, not a single person had come out in support of Maximillian Sutton.

Tristan had hugged him when he'd confessed this.

"Looks like my Ice Princess was actually a Queen all along, huh?" he'd teased. He'd pulled back and given James a levelheaded stare. "You should be more confident in yourself. You're an amazing manager and a role model for many artists. In fact, I think Eddie is crushing on you hard."

James had sniffed and burrowed his face in Tristan's shoulder, happiness overriding the anxiety churning his stomach.

"Eddie is cute, but he can't hold a candle to you. No man can."

"Damn," Tristan had muttered. "Now I really want to take you back to bed and ravish you."

They hadn't had sex last night. Instead Tristan had wrapped James in his arms and held him until he fell asleep.

James had looked at him from beneath his lashes and chewed his lip. "Why don't we do that? I think it will help me relax."

Tristan had groaned at his seductive tone. "You

know why we can't. Roman and the others are about to show up any minute now. I'm not having them catching us in flagrante delicto."

James's shoulders had knotted at his words.

Kurt had called half an hour ago to give him a warning shot.

"We're on our way over. Just so you know, Roman is royally pissed." His voice had hardened. "So are the rest of us. Lewis is practically spitting nails and you know that guy is normally as mild as a sloth."

Luckily, Drake had accompanied them. He and Tristan were the primary reasons things hadn't gone completely batshit crazy yet.

"Idiot," Lewis mumbled, his face flushed as he too glowered at James. "Nincompoop. Dingleberry."

Everyone stared at that last one.

"It's another word for dingbat," Lewis said sullenly.

Roman started pacing James's lounge. "When?" he grated out in the taut silence.

James looked at him.

Roman ground his teeth. "When did you sleep with that asshole?!"

"I—" James hesitated and lowered his gaze. "It was before your first national gig."

A deadly hush filled the room.

"What?" Hugo said hoarsely. "Are you saying the reason we landed a national tour was because you had sex with Maximillian Sutton?!"

"No!" James stopped and clenched his fists. "Look, it just expedited things. I—I didn't want you to miss that chance."

"I would rather Crazyknot have been a total failure than have you sell yourself to that asshole," Roman said flatly.

James shuddered and closed his eyes, shame weighing him down all over again.

"I know you're upset, but that was uncalled for," Tristan told Roman tightly.

"Tristan is right," Drake said quietly. "It's clear James regrets his actions and has lived with this guilt for years. You have to get over—" He stopped and drew a sharp breath.

James's head snapped up. His heart twisted.

Fat tears were rolling down Roman's ashen face.

"Roman," he mumbled, rising to his feet.

"Stop it!" Roman snapped.

James twitched.

Roman stormed up to him and grasped his cheeks in hot hands. "Stopping putting us ahead of yourself. Stop putting *me* ahead of your own needs and desires."

James's vision blurred.

Roman's chin wobbled. "I know I'm selfish and immature and I've made your life hell over the years, but it breaks my heart that you couldn't rely on me. That you couldn't rely on *us*."

Kurt sniffed and wiped his eyes. James realized all his friends were crying.

"I would gladly give up what we have today if it means erasing what happened to you in the past," Lewis blubbered. "All of us would. You're more important than Crazyknot, James."

He rose and came to hug James tightly.

James sobbed as Roman and the others closed their arms around them.

They stayed like that for a long time, their bodies shuddering as they shed heavy tears for the awful secret he'd had to bear on his own and what he'd lost.

"So, you and Tristan, huh?" Roman pulled back and wiped his snotty nose on the tissue Drake passed him. He looked curiously between them. "How long has that been going on?"

James blew his nose in the handkerchief Tristan gave him. "Over a month. We met the day you took me to see the Strickland Estate."

Roman's eyes rounded. "Oh. So when you said he fixed your car, you meant—?"

"He did fix my car," James protested.

Lewis chewed his lip, his eyes bright with curiosity. "What else did he do? Lou Lou wants deets."

Kurt pinched his cheek. "Behave."

He studied Drake and Tristan guardedly while Lewis peeled his fingers off his flesh and grumbled. "You know, you guys are awfully calm considering what's happening."

Drake shrugged. "When you've lived with the Terrible Seven for going on three decades, you get used to drama and tears."

"Remember when Izzy broke up with her first boyfriend?" Tristan grunted.

Drake grimaced. "My eardrums still haven't recovered."

James smiled. He startled a little when Roman hugged him again.

"I'm happy for you," Roman mumbled in the crook of his neck. "Also, if you need tips on how to take a big dick, let me know."

James flushed. "Hmm, I think I'm good on that front."

Lewis appraised Drake and Tristan with a shrewd stare. "So, who's got the bigger cock between the two of you?"

"Jesus Christ," Kurt groaned.

"Wow," Hugo mumbled.

Robbie waited with an expectant expression.

"Yeah, no," Tristan stated adamantly.

"I mean, there's an easy way to find that out." Lewis's gaze dropped to their crotch.

"We're not showing you our dicks," Drake said flatly.

"How're you finding the place?" Hunter asked Miles with a grin.

Miles looked warily around *The Watering Hole.* "It's...pretty cool."

Hunter grimaced. "Pretty cool?"

Color stained Miles's cheeks. He ducked his head and sipped his beer.

"Ignore him," Tristan grunted. "The way he talks this bar up, you'd think he owned it."

"Hey!" Hunter protested. "I'll have you know I have some pretty special memories of this place.' He winked at Theo.

Theo met their leaden stares. "We did not have sex here," he said flatly.

Hunter pouted. "We almost did."

Miles's face went bright red.

It was the first time he'd come out with them since he'd returned home. Though he looked more relaxed than the last time Tristan had seen him, they were aware all of this was still new to Miles. He'd lost a decade of his life and the world he'd awoken to was as unfamiliar as landing on the moon.

Movement near the door caught Tristan's gaze. His pulse quickened.

James had just walked in. A dazzling smile lit up his face when he spotted Tristan across the room.

Tristan's belly flip-flopped as he watched him make his way over.

"Dude, you are *so* whipped," Hunter teased.

To Tristan's surprise, the rest of the Terrible Seven had accepted his relationship with James without batting an eyelid. Carter had been especially pleased.

"It's about time the two of you found someone," the movie star had said. "Both of you deserve to be happy." He'd stopped and grimaced. "Especially James. I mean, I know I had it rough with Mira, but it must have been even worse for him."

Mira Peters was a former Hollywood movie producer Carter had had an affair with at the start of his career. It was only recently that the world had found out she'd been trying to blackmail Carter into resuming their relationship by threatening to expose the fact that he was gay. This was after he became Maisie's guardian and started going out with Elijah. The scandal that had followed had seen Mira lose her job and become shunned by the industry that once lauded her.

As for Maximillian Sutton, three more victims of the music producer's predatory behavior had contacted Crazyknot's lawyers in the aftermath of his arrest.

James had spent the following weeks dodging requests for interviews and ensuring the fallout didn't affect Crazyknot's upcoming album, all this under the close supervision of Roman and the rest of the band. They'd made it clear they wouldn't tolerate him covering their backs at his own detriment.

Tristan knew from his conversations with James that this was something he still needed to get used to. He'd spent half his life looking after his friends. Having them turn around and do the same to him was a novel experience.

James reached their table, dropped a kiss on Tristan's cheek, and took the seat beside him. He cast a curious look around. "Where's the rest of the gang?"

"I'm pretty sure Wyatt and Nathan are busy fucking again," Hunter grunted.

Miles looked like he wanted to crawl into the ground.

"Babe," Theo mumbled.

Drake sighed. "Carter and Elijah went out of town with Maisie. Alex and Finn are in Washington for an art exhibition. The rest of the stragglers will be here soon." He observed James steadily. "You look better than the last time I saw you."

"Thanks."

Izzy turned up half an hour later. Wyatt and Nathan weren't far behind her and did in fact look like they'd just had sex from the way their faces glowed. Tristan and Drake went to get everyone drinks and returned to find Izzy quizzing James about his relationship with Tristan.

"So, how'd the two of you hook up?" She grimaced and raised a warning hand. "And, please. I heard the story from Hunter. I'm not gonna accept that 'he fixed my car' bull."

"You don't need to answer that," Tristan told James firmly as he slipped into the seat beside him. "She's like a dog with a bone. It's best to ignore her."

James leaned back and fixed Izzy with a narrow-eyed stare. "But he did fix my car. He replaced my alternator and fuel filter."

The air sizzled as the pair studied one another.

"Whoa." Nathan's gaze swung between James and Izzy. "It's like Gunfight at the OK Corral."

"Don't encourage her," Wyatt groaned. "And I say that as her loving brother."

Hunter grinned. "Looks like Butterbeans has finally met her match, huh?"

Izzy flashed him an irritated look before skewering James with a piercing gaze. "So, is that what they're calling it these days?"

James blinked, nonplussed. "Calling what?"

Izzy glanced guilty at Miles. She leaned conspiratorially across the table.

"You know, a blowjob?!" She waggled her eyebrows. "'Replace your fuel filter?'"

Theo choked on his drink.

"Oh God," Miles mumbled.

"*Jesus, Izzy!*" Wyatt hissed.

"No, it isn't." Drake slammed a bottle on the table and scowled at Izzy. "And thanks. Now I'm gonna have that at the back of my mind every time Tristan fixes my truck."

Tristan's shoulders trembled.

"You okay?" James asked worriedly.

Tristan couldn't hold back anymore. He burst out laughing, the sound so loud it drew stares from the rest of the bar. James snorted. Then the whole table started laughing.

It was late by the time Tristan and James returned to the lodge. James grabbed an overnight bag from the trunk and placed his hand in Tristan's as they headed inside. Tristan took the bag off James, dropped it on the foyer floor, and pulled him into an embrace.

"I've missed you."

James clutched his back and burrowed his face in his shoulder. "I've missed you too. And I really like your friends."

"Even that pesky Izzy?"

James chuckled. "Yeah. Her heart's in the right place."

Tristan removed his glasses, tipped his chin up with a knuckle, and kissed him.

James sighed and melted against him.

Desire heated up their bodies as their hooded gazes locked. They fused their lips and tongues in a delicious play that soon had them hot and aching. Tristan let James go and tugged him inside the lounge. A dying fire glowed in the hearth, the light it emitted painting the room in shades of amber.

Tristan threw fresh logs on the smoldering flames, backed James against a wall, and started stripping him.

"Here?" James asked breathlessly, his eyes bright with excitement as he looked around the mellow space.

"Yeah."

James's hand found his rock hard cock through his jeans.

Tristan hissed.

"Is this one of your fantasies, Mr. Hart?" James nibbled on his jawline while he massaged Tristan's erection.

Tristan groaned and kissed him hard. "Shit! I want to be inside you!" he growled against his lips.

CHAPTER TWENTY-EIGHT

James panted as Tristan hastily undressed him and started taking care of his own clothes. He touched and kneaded Tristan's shoulders and arms and rained blistering kisses down his chest and abs while he got rid of his jeans and boxers, his heart racing.

Tristan groaned and tipped his head back when James lowered himself to his knees and teased his cock with clever flicks of his tongue. He braced his hands against the wall and breathed heavily as he watched James circle his slit with his tongue before sucking him inside his mouth.

James groaned, relishing Tristan's salty taste and his heat. He worked the silken skin and veins covering his shaft hungrily with his lips.

Tristan cursed when he took him to the back of his throat and started blowing him hard and deep. He tolerated the delicious torture for a minute before pulling his sensitive flesh out of the hot depths of James's mouth and yanking him to his feet.

James made a strangled sound as Tristan grasped his right leg, hooked it over his thigh, and rubbed their erections together.

He closed his eyes on a moan. "God! That feels *so* good!"

Tristan nudged his chin up and started kissing and biting his throat as they bumped and ground against one another. James's belly clenched violently when Tristan dropped a hand between their bodies and stroked his aching cock.

"*Ah!*" James gasped and punched his hips forward.

"Yeah, just like that!" Tristan growled. "Come for me!"

James scored marks on Tristan's biceps as he clung to him, his face tight with pleasure and his mouth open on throaty groans. A delicious tension knotted his belly all too soon and sent him over the edge. He stiffened and shouted out his pleasure as he climaxed, his cock pulsing hot cum all over Tristan's hand.

Tristan let go of him, spun him around, and dropped to his knees.

"Hands on the wall, James." He leaned it and sank his teeth in James's left ass cheek.

James shuddered at the sting and obeyed, still dizzy from his orgasm. The warm air made his hole twitch as Tristan parted his cleft and exposed his pucker. He moaned when Tristan slipped two slick fingers inside him and prepped his entrance.

James's spent cock twitched and swelled again as he cursed and writhed against Tristan's clever fingers.

Then Tristan brought his tongue into play and James fairly lost his mind.

Having Tristan rim him was hands down the most wicked thing he had ever experienced in his entire life. Hot tingles speared his insides as Tristan flicked, circled, and thrust inside his hole with his tongue.

Tristan ate and finger fucked him to a second, explosive climax that made his throat hoarse from shouting and had sweat dripping freely down his face. By the time Tristan slipped his fingers out of his quivering entrance, James was a trembling mess.

Tristan rose, twisted him around, and hooked his hands under his thighs. James gasped as Tristan lifted him up against his body. He wrapped his legs automatically around Tristan's hips and bit his lip on a moan when their erections brushed.

Tristan's eyes were feverish with lust as he positioned James for his penetration.

James hooked his arms around his neck and licked the sweat beading his nose. "Fuck me!" he panted.

Tristan made an animal sound and pressed the head of his cock against his opening. James gasped as he was stretched exquisitely open when Tristan pushed inside him.

"*Yes!*" He dropped his head back and canted his hips.

Tristan hissed when the angle allowed him to slide in more easily. He gritted his teeth and carefully pressed past the tight ring of muscles inside James.

James cried out as Tristan bottomed out on a deep groan.

They stilled, their breathing coming hard and fast.

James met Tristan's gaze as he started moving inside him. Fire licked at his veins at his wild expression. He sought Tristan's lips and swallowed his grunts as he took them on a savage ride.

James came once. Twice. Still Tristan moved, low hisses and curses tumbling from his mouth as James's convulsions massaged his erection. Movement caught James's eyes when he blinked his eyes open dazedly after his second climax. His breath caught.

He could see their reflection in the glass wall opposite.

Could see Tristan's ass and thighs contracting powerfully as he pumped his cock inside him. Could see the way he clutched Tristan's back wildly and marked his skin with his nails. Could see his untamed expression as he grunted and groaned, his body moving in perfect sync with Tristan's thrusts.

The carnal sight tipped him into his most powerful climax yet and pushed Tristan over the crest he'd been riding.

James's ears rang and his vision flickered as he came on a scream.

Tristan stiffened on a guttural shout, his cock throbbing violently as he ejaculated deep inside James. Dizzying pleasure stormed James's senses as they convulsed in each other's arms, his passage contracting so hard Tristan hissed as he found his pulsing cock being milked.

Tristan dropped his head back and squeezed his eyes shut as he grunted and rutted fitfully against him. James kissed the strong column of his throat and licked the sweat he found there, his insides full to bursting with Tristan's seed and his body quaking from the shattering orgasms Tristan had brought him to.

It felt like a lifetime before Tristan's awareness returned.

He panted heavily as he opened his eyes and met James's dazed stare.

James kissed him softly. "That was unreal."

Tristan cursed when he clenched his insides around his sensitive cock. He pulled out carefully and slid James down his body. James flushed as cum oozed out of his hole.

Tristan's eyes flared possessively.

"Let's get you cleaned up." He kissed James's knuckles and tugged him upstairs.

They showered, put on T-shirts and sweatpants, and were soon sitting comfortably in front of the fire. James sighed as Tristan wrapped a blanket around them where they'd settled on the hardwood floor.

He leaned his back against Tristan's chest. "This is bliss."

"Ah-huh." Tristan kissed his damp hair and hugged him closer.

Logs crackled in the cozy silence.

James trailed a finger up and down Tristan's left arm. "You know, I only have to be in L.A. once or twice a week."

Tristan stilled. He squeezed his arms around him. "I have a den I hardly use. It would make a great office."

James's finger froze. He looked over his shoulder

and met Tristan's steady gaze, his heart pounding. "It will?"

Tristan nuzzled his nose, his eyes twinkling in the light from the flames. "Yeah."

"Okay." He kissed Tristan and settled back in his arms, his entire body growing light with happiness.

Tristan hesitated. "Crazyknot—"

"Will accept it," James said in a firm voice. He lifted Tristan's hand and kissed his knuckles. "You're my number one now."

Tristan's chest shuddered with a tremulous breath. "Want to get hitched?"

James's stomach clenched. He pulled away and turned in Tristan's hold.

"You're gonna have to redo that proposal," he chided, struggling to keep a goofy smile from spreading across his face.

Tristan swallowed a chuckle.

"I want a candlelit dinner, roses, the works," James said adamantly.

"Do you now, Mr. Bossy Boots?" Tristan leaned it and nibbled on the side of his neck.

James shivered and hummed, eyes fluttering shut as he instinctively angled his head. They slammed open a second later. "Are you trying to distract me?"

Tristan laughed and tipped him onto his back. "What if I am?"

James bit his lip as Tristan settled in the cradle of his body. "Well, you're doing a very good job of it," he fake grumbled.

He hooked his arms and legs around Tristan and

leaned up to take his mouth in a scorching kiss. Tristan sighed as he sank into his embrace, the desire between them burning so bright it seared James's senses.

They made love late into the night and talked until dawn about their future. As they sat on Tristan's deck and watched the sun rise on a new day, James knew his life would never be the same again. And he'd never been more glad for it.

THE END

Miles Martinez is a man lost to the past. Can his new neighbor show him he still has a lot to live for?
Get Miles (Twilight Falls 7)

Have you read the Nights series yet? Find out if Gabe Anderson accepts Cam Sorvino's promise of one night of mindless pleasure to help him overcome his phobia of intimacy!
Get One Night (Nights 1)
Turn the page to read an extract now!

ONE NIGHT (NIGHTS #1) SPECIAL PREVIEW

WHAT THE HELL AM I DOING HERE?

Gabe Anderson scanned the crowded club in the mirror opposite the bar before looking down into his scotch with a self-deprecating smile. This had seemed like such a great idea an hour ago, when he'd been staring at an empty weekend in an even emptier apartment.

Saron was located in a side alley, a short walk from Shinjuku's main club strip. Despite its somewhat shady location, the place oozed style.

Gabe had hesitated when he'd seen the suited doorman guarding the entrance and wondered if access was by invitation only. He only knew of *Saron* from overhearing his clients mention it a few nights ago. From what he'd made of their excited conversation, it was *the* place to hang out in Shinjuku if you were of a particular sexual inclination.

The doorman had checked Gabe over for all of three seconds before wordlessly unclipping the rope from the stanchions framing the steel doors. He had obviously passed some kind of test, though what it was he didn't know.

Beyond a foyer with a cloakroom manned by a male attendant who looked like he'd walked straight out of a *GQ* shoot were a set of shallow steps leading to a wide, sunken floor.

Despite the butterflies churning his stomach, Gabe had stopped and stared appreciatively at the decor. As a consultant for one of Chicago's biggest design firms, he could tell how much money had gone into giving *Saron* its unique look. The club was drowned in deep reds, dark purples, and rich earth tones. Scattered across the oak floor were Brazilian cherry wood tables and armchairs boasting plush velvet upholstery and satin cushions. Discrete booths dotted the walls and afforded privacy to those who needed it, although the muted lighting provided enough of that as it was. A polished mahogany counter with wine-red leather and walnut stools ran the length of the bar on the right.

At the far end of the room, a woman in a black cocktail dress stood on a raised podium. She was crooning a song in a sultry, deep voice, her eyes closed and her glossy ruby lips glistening in the mellow spotlight. Behind her, cymbals vibrated gently, a piano tinkled, and a saxophone hummed, the sounds somehow rising above the voices of the men packing the place.

It was as he'd made his way to the bar that Gabe had realized why the doorman had let him in. From the looks of the club's patrons, *Saron* catered exclusively to an upscale clientele. He was willing to bet a week's wages none of the suits in the place cost less than five hundred dollars.

"Ah, fresh meat."

Gabe froze in the act of sitting on a barstool, his gaze swinging up to meet a pair of amused green eyes on the other side of the mahogany counter.

"Excuse me?" he said stiffly.

The bartender, a striking blond in a slate, silk tuxedo vest and crisp white shirt, flashed him a grin.

"I've not seen you around these parts before. What will it be?"

Gabe swallowed, wondering whether the man had seen straight through him and grasped the reason he had come to *Saron*.

"What will what be?" he mumbled, unable to mask the apprehension in his voice.

The bartender pursed his lips and observed him with a shrewd expression before leaning across the counter.

"Relax," he murmured in Gabe's left ear. "I can tell it's your first time in a place like this. If you keep up that deer-in-the-headlights look you've got painted across that pretty face of yours, you're gonna be a target for every sleaze ball in this club. And, trust me, they might be wearing thousand-dollar ensembles, but some of these assholes are nothing but dirty pigs in suits."

An involuntary bark of laughter left Gabe's lips at the mental image the bartender's words had conjured. The sound carried along the counter, drawing stares.

The knot of tension that had been sitting between Gabe's shoulder blades ever since he ventured into Shinjuku eased as he smiled at the bartender.

"I've never been called pretty before."

The guy winked.

"Trust me, you're the hottest thing on legs in this place right now. Besides me, of course."

Gabe chuckled and ordered a scotch, his confidence boosted by the compliment.

Two months had passed since he'd relocated to Tokyo from Chicago. When his bosses had sprung the offer on Gabe in early spring, the chance of a fresh start in a place void of the dark memories that had plagued him for eight years was too much of an attractive proposition for him to reject. He'd left Chicago with two suitcases and five crates full of books and artwork, the only things he had to show after a decade in the city.

Though he had been prepared for the culture shock, life in Tokyo had still come as a surprise, albeit an invigorating one. He had always had an interest in the country and its intoxicating mix of traditional and contemporary customs ever since he made his first business trip to the Japanese branch of the firm four years ago.

Luckily, his new position suited him to a T. He had thrown himself into his first assignment with his usual drive and passion, leading the team under him to make good on a project, one which his predecessor had only made a half-assed attempt to complete. He had delivered on time, on budget, and on schedule, despite the nearly impossible deadline. The crazy hours and weekends he had put in had not gone unnoticed, and the praise lavished on his team at the grand opening of their client's luxury hotel earlier that week was all the acknowledgment Gabe needed to realize he had made the right choice in moving to this city. The fact that the money he was making could easily afford him a two-bedroom condo in the exclusive neighborhood of Meguro didn't hurt, either.

Yet, despite having relocated thousands of miles to the other side of the world, his mind would not let go of the bite of his past. Which was why, when faced with the prospect of his first free weekend and the boxes he had yet to unpack, he had looked up *Saron*'s location on the spur of the moment and decided to take a gamble.

He had promised himself this move would not be just a fresh start for his mind, but for his body, too. That he would start taking risks in his personal life again. That he would not let the bastard who had made it impossible for him to ever have a satisfying physical relationship win.

Fifteen minutes into his first drink and Gabe wondered whether he had made a bad choice. So far, Ethan, the bartender, had helped him field a burly, yakuza-looking type with tattoos up the side of his neck, three old men with sweaty palms and bald patches, and a couple of young guys who looked barely past the legal age of drinking.

With his lean build, dark hair, and blue eyes, Gabe knew he was an attractive prospect. Add in that he was a foreigner and he was coming to the conclusion that he had become a beeline for all the men in the bar who wanted to make a conquest out of the white guy – a white notch in the proverbial bedpost. They all wanted to fuck him or be fucked by him.

A cynical half-smile twisted his lips at that thought. If only they knew.

He raised a hand to the back of his neck and rubbed the warm spot that had been bothering him for a while. Something made him look up from his drink then – call it instinct or that subconscious voice that warns of imminent danger. Movement in the mirror opposite the bar caught his gaze. Or, more precisely, a lack of it.

Stormy gray eyes pierced him from the other end of the club. They locked on him, a beam of light in the gloom. Transfixing him. Immobilizing him.

Gabe's breath caught in his throat, every muscle in his body tightening in fight-or-flight mode.

The man sat apart from the crowd, alone at a table that could have accommodated three, a tumbler full of dark liquid clasped casually in his left hand. His red silk tie was crooked, as if he had slipped a finger through the knot to loosen it. The top two buttons on his white shirt were open, revealing tan skin covering toned muscles and a hint of curls.

Gabe couldn't tell whether his hair was dark brown or dirty blond. It was hard to say in the dim light. What wasn't hard to see were the subtle and not-so-subtle stares the other men in the bar were giving the stranger.

With his stubbled face, smoldering looks, and what appeared to be an incredibly ripped body beneath a custom-tailored charcoal suit, the man looked like a king sitting on a throne, commanding a roomful of servants. Servants who appeared more than willing to either get fucked by him or fuck him if he so much as lifted his little finger.

And a man like that would not have to ask twice.

Envy and irritation flashed through Gabe at that thought, shattering the spell he found himself under. He broke eye contact, shocked by the feelings suddenly flooding him, and glared at his half-empty glass. It seemed to mock him, as if it were a reflection of his own life. A half-empty, broken shell. Incapable of touching someone or to be touched.

Gabe lifted the glass and downed the rest of the drink with an angry flick of his wrist. Fire singed his throat. He welcomed the burning sensation, hoping it would calm the pounding in his chest and the tightness in his belly and groin that told him his body had reacted to the stranger.

A full glass of scotch appeared next to his empty tumbler.

Gabe looked up at Ethan, puzzled.

A remorseful grimace flashed across the bartender's face. "Looks like we're no longer the two hottest bastards in this joint. Here, compliments of the King."

Gabe stared at the drink before slowly looking over his shoulder, his pulse picking up speed.

Gray Eyes raised his glass in a toast. A teasing smile played on his sculptured lips before he knocked back his drink.

You're kidding me.

Gabe tried to block out the heated tingle running across his skin at the stranger's cocky smirk and the way his powerful throat muscles worked when he swallowed. He turned to Ethan.

"That's his *actual* name?"

Ethan grunted. "Well, no. But the asshole sure acts like one."

There was movement in the mirror opposite Gabe.

Read One Night today

AFTERWORD

To all my friends who helped make this possible. You know who you are.

To you, my readers. Thank you for reading Tristan and James's story. I hope you loved the sixth book in the Twilight Falls series. I would be grateful if you could leave a review on Goodreads or on the store where you purchased this book. Reviews help readers like you find my books and I truly appreciate your honest opinions about my stories.

Make sure to sign up to my store newsletter for special deals on my books and new release alerts. Or you can sign up to my author newsletter instead to get upcoming release notifications, sneak peeks, and giveaways.

BOOKS BY A.M. SALINGER

Nights

One Night - 1

The Escort - 2

Tokyo Heat - 3

Sweet Obsession - 4

Sweet Possession - 5

The Proposition - 6

Undisclosed - 7

Hush - 8

One Day - 9

Twilight Falls

Alex - 1

Carter - 2

Hunter - 3

Wyatt - 4

Drake - 5

Tristan - 6

Miles - 7

ABOUT THE AUTHOR

Ava Marie Salinger is the romance pen name of an Amazon bestselling author with a passion for writing addictive tales. Known for her action-packed and thrilling urban fantasy novels, she has expanded her repertoire with the introduction of the M/M urban fantasy romance series Fallen Messengers. Additionally, she has penned the scorching hot contemporary M/M romance series Nights and Twilight Falls as A.M. Salinger. When not immersed in her writing, Ava can be found curating inspiring music playlists, indulging in her love for nature, marveling at the latest gadgets, and savoring Chinese cuisine.

You can find all of Ava's books on her author store at shop.adstarrling.com